Short stories

by

Mike Lees

Collection of short stories by

Mike Lees

Outpost

Science fiction

Gar, an alien, at home in the distant Core of Systems at the centre of the Galaxy, has become a 'Terrorist' by necessity. Caught up within a corrupt system of power struggles and deceit, he must find his path to redemption and revenge. But when he is caught in an act of thievery, with two other complices, Gar is banished to a far Outpost. He spends his time collating information on Humans and their society and values. Resigned to years of outcast life, an opportunity arises when an exploration vessel from Earth visits the Outpost...

Albia

Fantasy

At odds with her schoolmates and a self-inflicted drought on social media, Albia is alone, lost even. An underlying sense of anticipation gnawing at her.

Until one day she receives a massage. She'd say later, a calling. An answer to her yearning? Can she assume her destiny? Will she find the happiness, love and purpose she yearns for? Or will the dark forces destroy her chance of finding contentment?

The Fox

Psychological fantasy

Follow John, a family man, in his adventure into the Scottish Highlands to find answers to his increasing sense of loss in a world he feels is overtaking him and destroying the love he once had. Can John find his inner-self, contentment of the mind and body? Will the Fox be able to help him? And who is the Fox?

Semper Supra

Military science fiction

Earth is visited by an alien force determined to cripple the human race. They believe Humans represent a danger to their status quo in the Spiral Arm in which Earth occupies. Can the newly formed United States Space Force do anything to repel the attack? Chris, a Space Guardian, part of the US Military forces, participates in the Guardian's first test at protecting Earth. Can they succeed against all odds? And do competing countries on Earth pit together to ensure success? Find out in this exciting new novella presenting the new and untried Space Guardians.

Outpost

Mike Lees

Chapter 1

Sneak, Sneak

Gar fretted as he wiled away the time in his meagre living quarters. Another two hours to go. He glanced over to Hatch, who was fiendishly swiping at his slate. Latia was busy in the kitchen preparing a snack. She too was biding her time. It was hanging on them like rain on a freezing day.

"Are you sure this plan is ok?" said Gar.

Hatch looked up from his slate, "You talking to me?"

"Well, you're the brains. I imagine you've got everything nailed down, eh?"

"Like a coffin, my friend. Can't go wrong. Just do your part, we'll do ours and it'll be sunny skies all the way."

"Yeah, all the way to prison if it was anything like last time. Fortunate for us, my superior intelligence saved the day."

"Listen Ugar'Philde, those are the risks of being a terrorist. Who would have guessed the Princess was in bed with her servant? She was supposed to be alone, sleeping. And what happens? Her lover took a fire pick to us. Lucky he didn't want to be caught either. I don't see where your 'superior intelligence' came into it," said Hatch, fumbling with his slate.

"I recognized the gameplay and the problems he would get into and negotiated a deal. As for the Princess, well, she was hardly in a position to do much," he finished chuckling.

"Yeah, that was mega."

"What are you two boys sniggering about," Latia said, shuffling in with a plate of sugar-coated mumfs.

"Oh, good, grub."

"Not for you," she said, then turned to Hatch, "Nor you. These are merit only. No mess-ups tonight ok?"

"Calm down, lovely, I have it under control. My plan is par excellence."

"Par excellence? What does that mean?" she said.

"It means you can relax. I have the plans of the Ambassadors' premises in here," he said, tapping his head.

"That's what's worrying me. You know you don't function at the best of times."

All three spent the wait, each one to their ways. Hatch, deep into his slate. Latia, scoffing away at her mumfs and Gar, getting lost in his thoughts.

He'd become a terrorist two sun cycles ago when his brother was killed by two corrupt policemen who, after killing him in cold blood, had planted incriminating evidence. They were neck deep in a drug traffic, along with the Chief of police and two local politicians. Despite publically condemning the destruction the drugs were doing among the youth, they were secretly part of the chain of command behind the scenes. The justice found his brother guilty and condemned posthumously. This was often the practice; putting the burden on the families and companions of such individuals. This allowed the police to harass them. The slightest misdemeanour and they would be up for trial for drug trafficking. All the while, politicians and members of the police force were creaming off the proceeds for their own personal gain.

In fact, many departments of Government were corrupt and took bribes, allowing the gangs to freewheel. A few brave journalists tried to bring the corruption to light, but were often accused of hyped up charges that would either get them killed or put in prison for many years. The entire system was working for itself, leaving the population to suffer and lose hope.

Yes, a terrorist. It was his vocation. He was sure.

The Ambassador represented a drug producing country and facilitated their transport via his diplomatic pouch. A pouch, that more often than not, comprised five or six pallets rather than a small bag of goods. The 'pouch' swam through customs like a Swan on a summer's day. He had documents in his safe that would prove the corruption, and that is what they were after.

Time crept by, but like anything else, it made its way to when they had to go.

"Right, everybody, let's go. Gar, got your stuff for the service door?" asked Hatch.

"Of course. I'll get us in, no worries."

Hatch stared at him an instant, "Right. Latia, get that robe on and some makeup. You need to be seductive, darling. Like I know you can be," he added with a wink.

"Shut up, you shitbag. You wouldn't know seductive even if it slapped you in the face. I'm doing this for the job, ok?"

"Yeah, yeah, I know. Get ready anyway."

Ten minutes later, they all piled into their car. Gar drove to within a mile of the premises. "Right, it's eleven o'clock. Everyone should be in bed, or at least dozing somewhere or drunk. I'll park the car here. We can do the rest by foot."

They waked up to the wall surrounding the premises, each one some distance apart so as not to arouse any suspicion. A couple of dim street lights cast useful shadows through the row of trees lining the road. Hatch caught up to Gar, "You sure you can handle that safe? You got the decoder? You know the model, right?"

"Calm down, I know what I am doing. Eh, what safe?" said Gar.

"What do you mean 'what safe'? We talked about it several days ago. You said you can break it, no problem," said Hatch, worried.

"Oh that, yes well eh, my decoder for the back door should do that as well. Take it easy."

"Fuck you Gar, if you mess up this time, you're out."

"Big words for a small man. Anyway, leave it to me. Oh, here we are," Gar said as they neared the service door in the exterior wall. He heard scuffing and looked up, "What is Latia doing? She's climbing the wall! The cameras!" said Gar.

They ran up to the wall, gesturing for her to come down. They also got a good look up her robe. "Get down, you idiot. We mentioned nothing about climbing the wall. Gar here has a decoder for the door."

"Oh, yeah, right, I forgot," she said as she let herself drop onto the pavement.

"Shit Latia, concentrate. Gar, get that door open and don't set the alarms off ok?"

"What a question. You know me," Gar said as he slid a small electronic box out of his bag trailing three wires, "Right, let me have a look at this beauty."

Seconds later, the door clicked open. They all listened for any alarms or commotion in the building further away. Nothing. All seemed quiet.

"Good, let's hope your trick shut the cameras off. Ok let's go. Our entrance door is to the right, fifty yards away. You go first, Gar?" said Hatch.

"Me, why me? I'm the tech guy. You're the super athlete hero," said Gar in the gloomy shade of the trees lining the wall.

Hatch rolled his eyes and jogged toward the building. Latia and Gar followed with a crouch run. Hatch and Gar both bent to look at the lock on the veranda door when they heard a pop! They both jumped and looked around. Latia was popping bubble gum. "Shit Latia, keep quiet," said Hatch as he turned back to Gar fiddling with the lock, "Any chance?"

"Yep, nearly there," then a click and the door gently swung open. Gar put his hands across the entrance to block Hatch, who wanted to enter. "There are sensors around the door. Give me two ticks to disable them," he then connected two cables to one sensor and a third to a cable running across the door plinth. "Am I not good?" he said smugly as he gestured for them to go through.

Once they were inside, the lights came on...

Before them stood five guards. The Ambassador stepped through them to confront the trio in his pyjamas.

* * *

The trial took place three weeks later. They presented all three before the judge for sentencing. The trial lasted ten minutes with no legal representation.

The judge, an elderly woman with grey greasy hair, looked down upon them. "Miss Latia, in view of your young age and gullible nature, I favour a lenient approach to your punishment. I shall send you to Gol'gath to undergo rehabilitation with the sisters there until deemed fit for society. You, Sir," she said, glaring at Hatch, "In view you are the, what shall we say, 'Mastermind' and oldest member of this group," she said with a smirk, "I sentence you to five years hard labour on the mining planet Holl'nath." Gar looked over to his friend, whose ears were swept back at hearing the news. Holl'nath. Few convicts returned and most stayed for life despite the brevity of their punishment, some died. It was a one-way ticket to hell. Gar took in a gasp as the Judge looked at him.

"As for you, young man, in view of your age and weak mind I feel, like Miss Latia here, that you should undergo some rehabilitation. I have something special for you. You are to be shipped to Outpost 751 to monitor Earth. Earth is a planet that is just emerging from a neo-industrial age and has showed a penchant for violence. The Outpost is very near this planet and is our major source of data concerning the inhabitants. Close surveillance is necessary, and I am convinced it will enable you to see the misguidance they have sadly subjected you to of recent. A superior will supervise you and shall report periodically. However, I feel urged to give you a choice. You can also occupy a stasis chamber for three years. Tell me what you choose, now."

Gar looked to his friends, agape, "Eh, the Outpost I guess," he mumbled.

Chapter 2

"What in the blazes is that?"

Constellation: Centaurus

Star system: Alpha Centauri

Star: Proxima Centauri

Planet: Proxima Centauri C

Spacecraft: Earth Ship CEV-002 Vanity

Mission: explore the system's planets for a potential scientific outpost implantation

Distance from Earth: 4.24 light years

Date: 2080

"Stop gawking Mr Stone and get this ship aligned, we're out of our orbital contingency," said Vanity's Captain, Gerald Derrick as he stalked around the bridge like a captured lion.

"What in the blazes is that?" Jones gasped, peering at his sensor console.

"Control yourself, Mr Jones," cautioned Derrick.

"Yessir. Sorry, sir. It's surprising. Sunlike radioactive readings from merely a pinpoint."

Derrick watched the vid screen showing planetside and wondered what had caught Jones's attention. Their mission was scientific; to scout the Alpha Centauri System for a workable site to install a permanent scientific station. They were orbiting one of the three planets, the most promising. They started a survey of the surface the day before. It was a dull landscape showing few seas but plenty of large lakes, a few mountainous regions, with perpetual ice on both poles, while the equator had a desert climate. The planet having no tilt of its axis, those zones were stable, either permanently frozen or continuously hot and dry. No notable animal life, but vegetation in the intermediary zones. It was already promising until they discovered the anomaly...

* * *

Derrick frowned as he pored over the images of the area in question, a little north of the equator. Sensors showed a bright spot, about one kilometre in diameter, of significant radioactive emissions, stable and intense. Sand storms hindered visuals, although they could determine a desolate land in the immediate area. "Zoom in," commanded Derrick.

"Aye, Sir," responded Jones.

The image blinked out, then came back, a small black circle in the middle. Derrick thought it was a pixel error until a refresh of the image still presented a black circle. He let out a gasp. No reflections showed up on the objet, just a black circle on the planet's surface. "Diameter? Can we get a side view?"

"Not in our present geostationary orbit. We must move off it to get a side view," Jones said, "Its reading 40 metres in diameter."

"Mr Stone, move up ahead of that thing, say 15 degrees," ordered Derrick to the navigation officer and pilot Mr Stone.

"Aye Aye Sir. Starting maneuver now."

Derrick felt the ship pulsate as it surged forward.

"Coming up to a 15 degree change in relation to the object in 2.35 minutes, Sir," informed Stone.

Moments later Jones exclaimed, "Good lord, it's a tower or… spike. Readings say it's 828 metres high!"

Derrick, eyes wide, could not believe what he was seeing. A slender in-curving spike finishing into infinity rose from the barren land with no discernible sign of any other edifice around the object. Derrick pressed the comm button. "Professor Hadley, are you getting this?"

"Indeed, we are, Captain Derrick, absolutely stunning. We are all having babies down here in the lab! We need to go down with a team immediately."

Derrick sighed, "First, it'll be night-time in 2 hours planetside so we must wait until sunrise in…," he looked to Stone who held up his ten fingers, "Ten hours," he glanced at the clock on the bulkhead, "That means 0830 ship time tomorrow. Second, as Captain, I decide when and where and what we do. Is that clear Professor Hadley?"

"As you wish Gerry, wouldn't want to upset your little boat."

Damn those scientific types. Derrick thought. It had been a continual struggle to keep discipline on the ship as the scientific contingent was not used to space command discipline and were apt to do as they thought. *Thank god we're here now. they've been idle too long,* mused Derrick. "That'll do Professor, no need to get touchy. A lack of discipline and order is a sure way to get us all killed out here. Be ready to disembark at 0830. Only four people, as I want to send a security detachment to accompany you. Captain out." Hoping that would end the discussion.

"But Gerry, we've already discussed this, I need my entire team with me. It is what we are here for, for chrissake. Four people are by far not enough. And our equipment, we'll need a whole shuttle just for us."

"Hadley, this is our first landing. Preliminary incursion. Safety first. Security is going with you. Now shut up and be ready in the morning," replied Derrick, slamming the comms button with frustration.

That shipside night, many slept, but little.

Chapter 3

Landing party

Captain Derrick said that he wanted Star Stone to pilot the shuttle planetside. 'You're level-headed, you'll be an asset down there.' Stone didn't know what to think of that but was glad for the opportunity to go down to the planet. Once everything loaded and everybody secured, Stone eased the shuttle through the bay doors and guided the vessel downward toward Proxima Centauri C, the official name of the planet. Silence pervaded the living space of the shuttle as everyone was looking through the front windows as the planet grew nearer. After some high atmosphere buffeting, shedding speed rapidly, they landed softly, the inertia drive being infinitely incremented to allow fine "in atmosphere" handling. Wanting to proceed with caution, Stone had landed approximately five hundred metres from the spike. Aboard the shuttle were the four guards and four lab techs that included Professor Hadley. The guards had been going stir crazy after several months cooped up in the Vanity. They all clumsily moved around the cabin in anticipation of getting out and seeing the planet's surface for real.

The suits and helmets over their anti-radioactive coveralls hindered any fluid motion. Captain Perez, the guard's leader, ordered Star to remain in the shuttle while the others scout the surface and immediate surroundings. So eight bulky beings lumbered out of the airlock, one at a time, which took fifteen minutes in all.

The radiation was of little concern, but caution prevailed near an unknown object, despite their protection. As they got out, Stone leaned against the windows to look down at them in their cumbersome suits. Strange beings in a strange land. He looked up to the Spike towering above them; the dust blocking the base from view, a truly alien presence, he thought, as he took in the stark obsidian black object standing out against the dim sky. Was it his imagination or did he feel the object through some esoteric primal sense? This was his first time planetside except Earth and the Moon and the sensation of being on an Earth-like planet but not quite gave him an all too unexpected sense of insecurity. It reminded him, starkly, that they were out on a limb. The slightest of errors could spell death. He saw drifts of dust when one or other of the team kicked the earth. The gravity, not quite earthlike at 0.87, made him feel lighter, even in the cockpit. He looked at the team who now stood stock still, probably mouths gaping, staring at the Spike, letting the shock set in. Black and ominous, they too felt its presence like a spider crawling up your back. It struck Stone that in this completely alien world; it was they who were the aliens, a sort of unnatural intrusion upon a quintessential landscape so so far from home. Star opened up the comms to the team so he could hear the chatter and follow events in real time. "Ok boys, let's get that trolley out and load up," he heard Hadley giving orders to his team of young scientists.

"Not so quick, Hadley," barked Perez through the suit's intercom, "We first scout the area before you lot start your experiments. Stone can come in with the shuttle when I am satisfied there is no danger."

Hadley rolled his eyes, thankful the visor was hiding his face, "as you wish, Herr Oberkommando."

"Shut it, Hadley, use comms only when necessary," quipped Perez, his glare hidden by his visor. He ordered two of his team, Draxler, a slim catlike yet hard-edged woman, known for her expertise with knives and Dellmayer, an affable yet capable American, to accompany him ahead and instructed the fourth guard, Kovitz, a hardened veteran from the messy and costly Mexican incursion, to close their backs. Kovitz was by far the meanest of the guards, having already suffered some disciplinary measures from the Captain during the journey. He'd continually goaded the science guys and never gave in to reason and often drew out one of his knives, hidden up his sleeve, to frighten anyone who didn't agree. The lab boys steered clear of him when they could in the tight confines of the ship. It would be fair to say that between the guards and lab boys there was no love lost and a quiet, under the surface, defiance blossomed between the two parties. Some would say, especially Hadley, that having four armed personnel with rifles was overkill. They were not expecting any danger except from the local wildlife, which did not seem to be an immediate danger. The surrounding area appeared desolate as the group moved toward the Spike while Stone checked communications, ensuring full comms with Vanity. The three other scientists were Jackson, a sort of Indiana Jones geologist, Darby, a strange and eccentric British guy specialising in micro-biology and finally a very excited assistant to

Professor Hadley, Carting, eyes wide at everything he saw. No one could blame him, being on this planet was fabulous, everyone was permanently doe eyed. Visibility was poor through the windswept terrain but when Stone looked up, he could make out the strange colours of the atmosphere even though it was early dawn. It must be a surface wind, only a few metres high, he thought. Proxima Centauri, the local flare star, was just coming up over the horizon. From space it looked quite bright, although somewhat darker than Earths. The emitting flares gave it an irregular pulsating appearance. The sky, an amazing purple and rose, gave a Disney World like backdrop to the alien landscape despite the sand storm. Temperature was around 35°C with a strong gusty wind, making horizontal visibility limited to twenty metres. The party trudged forward and was soon out of sight. Professor Hadley continued to complain through the helmet's comms, but everyone, including Stone, ignored him. Stone reported to the Vanity confirming the situation, and that they had set out for the Spike, which they now all called it.

Stone could see their advance by transponders on everyone's suits, but also via the vid feeds that equipped each helmet. He settled in facing the array of small screens, each showing the feed from every member of the team simultaneously. He expected them to reach the Spike in fifteen minutes at most. However, after only a couple of minutes, Perez called in on his private channel, "Stone, you sure we're going in the right direction. We've been trudging through this desert for an hour already? We still can't see anything. You said it was only five hundred metres from the shuttle."

"What do you mean? You've been on the way just over two minutes? According to your transponders, you've gone at least one hundred metres and in the right direction."

"Well, something's not right here. We've been putting up a good pace and those lab guys are already moaning"

Stone rubbed his chin a moment, "Could be the Spike interfering with my sensors, but all your feeds are showing up in the same pattern that you left with. Three of you up front, the four labs techs and one of your men at the rear."

"Ok, I'll see what Hadley thinks of it. He knows we should be there by now. We all saw the Spike when we landed. Not that far. I'll call when we arrive. Out."

"Roger, Stone out," he said as he monitored the readouts, but again two minutes later Hadley came on the general chatter band.

"Stone, how long have we been travelling from your point of view?"

My point of view? Thought Stone. "Eh, four and half minutes. And you?"

"Two and half hours. Are you sure we are going in the right direction?"

"Yes, you are, I have you all on my monitors showing normal progress."

Hadley coughed into the helmet's mic, "Well, it seems something is playing with space time here. The nearer we get, the further is it away. I'll be really grateful to get to that Spike and have a proper look. This is really taxing."

Kovitz snorted into his mic, "This is field work sonny boy, not yer comfy lab back at home. This is what you all signed up for or what?"

"Fucking weenies, if you ask me," added Draxler.

"Hey chick, take it easy on them folks, they ain't done no harm," threw in Dellmayer over the comms.

"Professor Hadley, are we lost?" sounded a wrought Jackson. "I mean, we're surely going in the wrong direction."

"I think lost is not the right word," interjected Carting. "I would say befuddled. The unexpected, which thankfully, is what we are here for; into the unknown and all that."

"When do we rest up? This suit is weighing me down and it stinks in here. A break would be nice," commented Darby.

"Shut the fuck up Darby, we've only just left. Boss? Do we have to put up with this? I hate babysitting," Kovitz sighed.

"That'll do everybody. Our job is to look after Hadley and his team. They're not expected to be tough. That's our job, so keep alert and your eyes open. Is that understood people?"

Three reluctant, yet distinct 'Yessir' came from Perez's team.

"Perez here. Damn Stone, if this continues we'll need you to come in. My men are ok, but the lab guys are taking it hard in this storm and heat. I'll call if we need you. In the meantime, be ready to lift off. Out."

"Roger that Captain. Stone out."

After a further three hours trudge, Perez opened on the comms, "Stone, we've arrived. Took us over six hours to get here. Hadley, what's happening? How come it took us so long to cover five hundred metres?"

"Indeed, a strange effect, which I would surmise is quantum fallout from the Spike. Time and space dilation the nearer we get. Amazing really! Back home, quite a few theoreticians had suggested a similar effect is possible on a quantum scale."

Hadley was in lecture mode, so Perez cut in, "lovely, so what does that mean to us and our ship? In simple terms, Hadley."

"Hmm, there are no simple terms, but the Spike is altering the space/time envelope around it. I would suppose our shuttle is just outside its influence. To know more, we need to study this object thoroughly. Just by looking at it will not get us far, indeed with the quantum effect, rather the contrary. We need our equipment, which is in the shuttle by the way," Hadley jibed.

Ignoring the remark, Perez gave orders to his three companions to scout around the base of the Spike and report if they encountered anything in particular. Hadley's team approached the Spike, now towering over them. "Absolutely intriguing. So smooth and slippery to the touch," muttered Hadley, "Jackson, any ideas, you're the geologist?"

"Without my scanners, I can't determine the nature of this object," Jackson said laconically, looking at Perez who was standing not two metres away, an impassive statue in his suit. He gave no reaction to Jackson's taunt.

"Captain, would it be possible for Stone to come in with the shuttle? We need our equipment," Hadley asked.

"Wait for my people to finish their scout and we'll see."

At that moment, Kovitz came into view through the sandstorm, "All clear as far as I can tell. Draxler and Dellmeyer went out further to do a larger tour."

"Very well," said an impatient Perez, feeling the unseen stares from Hadley and his team.

A few moments later, Draxler and Dellmeyer came into view, "Sir, we found a low artificial wall surrounding a ramp. We couldn't see that far in and we didn't want to venture further without additional support," Dellmeyer said.

"No sign of recent activity?"

"No, sir."

"Very well, Stone, did you get all that?"

"Yes, I did. Does that mean I am clear to approach?"

"Indeed, you are. Come in slowly. Home in on our transponders."

"Roger that Sir. Coming in," Stone said excitedly.

"A ramp?" exclaimed Hadley.

Chapter 4

The Spike

It took Stone twenty-five minutes to make it to the Spike, despite the good speed he'd made when he got above the sandstorm. When he arrived, he said, "Strange, I could see the Spike as I approached, but it seemed to get further away as I drew closer. A weird inside-out feeling."

"That'll be the quantum effect. Perception alters when you look at it. It works on the subjective mind. Can wreak havoc with your sensory organs. Here, it seems to have an actual effect on reality," commented Hadley as he approached the shuttle, eager to get his equipment from the shuttle's hold.

"Fucking weird shit if you ask me?" Kovitz said, giving a hand to open the hold's outside door.

"Keep a lid on it, Kovitz. Concentrate and stay alert. Dellmayer, give him a hand with those cases," Perez looked around, "Draxler, patrol duty at twenty metres distance from our position. Report as and when necessary. We'll look at that ramp in due course."

A couple of hours later the storm had abated, leaving the frail and pulsating sun to soak the ground in an eerie, diffused light. Hadley and his team had made several tests and probes of the Spike. They even chipped away a sample for microscopic examination, but were at a loss to determine the exact nature of the edifice. Hadley walked up to Perez, who was talking to Kovitz and Dellmayer. When he arrived, they saluted Perez and left snappishly. Hadley did not miss the contempt, "So what do you have, Hadley?" said Perez.

"Well, it is indeed a quantum entity."

"Entity?"

"Entity, inasmuch that is does not rely on normal universal physics. It's independent of its surroundings. Moreso, it is even influencing it, as we have seen when we approached. Hence entity. Although certainly not sentient. The object is mineral but laden with exotic particularities. The radiation has completely saturated it. Molecular examination shows little lest to say it's a mineral alloy. Certainly produced, not natural."

"I can see it's not natural, Professor. I don't need a PhD to see that."

Sighing, Hadley continued, "What I wanted to highlight is that it is only a part of a greater whole. I suspect the workings, or whatever, are underground. Oh, and the Spike is hollow. Apart from that, nothing else to note. I would say it's more like a funnel or channelling device, to what or of what, I do not know at present."

"Well, fucking great. I guess our next step is to investigate that ramp Draxler found," Perez paused a moment and made a movement to rub his chin but relinquished the idea, remembering his helmet, "Ok, pack up your stuff and be ready in one hour to proceed further. You may go back to the shuttle if you need to replenish your suit's water and feeding reserves," Perez did not wait for Hadley to reply before turning away to address Draxler, who was standing nearby.

An hour and fifteen minutes later, they were all gathered at the edge of the ramp, looking down. It was at least five metres wide with a gradual slope. "Can't see fucking hell down there!" shouted Kovitz over the comms. They all looked down toward the dark tunnel leading downward.

"Ok everybody, this is how it is going to go. Kovitz, you stand guard here. Keep the shuttle in view at all times and do regular patrols. You will monitor the main comms console here. Dellmayer, ensure you place comms relays every twenty metres as we penetrate inside. You will keep our rear along with Stone. Draxler and myself will take point," he looked at his team for confirmation, then saw Stone move up to him.

"Why me, I'm no good down there, I'm a pilot. I..."

Perez interrupted, "You're no use guarding the shuttle, I'd prefer Kovitz to handle that part and who knows what we find down there. Any point of view, as varied as they come, is welcome," he then turned away from Stone to stare at Hadley, "Professor Hadley, what are all those cases you've lugged here?"

"It's our equipment. We're going to need them for sure. We have our Spectrum analysis sensor and mobile chemical lab including a state-of-the-art InfraRed and UltraViolet deep scanner and acoustics, radioactivity and tremor apparatuses. Carting has bought along a very nice electro/quantum microscope and matter breakdown analysis projector meter. It's a beauty," rambled on Hadley.

"Stop right there! This is a strict minimum operation. This is our first incursion. We can always come back. No unnecessary junk in unknown territory."

Hurt, the Professor's voice became high pitched, "Junk? Mr Perez, this is science and we are a scientific expedition. You are here, to enable and protect us as and when necessary."

Perez held up his hand, "No reading off mission parameters, Professor! I have sufficient leeway in deciding our actions. If you think I'll adhere to something written out by some post doc fresh from college with absolutely no experience of what we are doing, then you're wrong. Take only what is necessary. The other stuff you can pile up over there, away from this ramp," he finished, pointing to a position a few metres away.

Jackson let out an audible sigh of relief, "Thank god for that. The thought of lugging all this around already started me sweating, and it's a stew tub in my suit as it is!"

"I second that! I could do with a shower like right now!" added Darby to what was fast becoming a tense situation.

Hadley thought for a moment then said with placating hands, "Very well, Mr Perez, you are perhaps right. I was getting carried away with my enthusiasm. Ok team, let's keep it to a minimum like the excellent Captain says." Nobody moaned.

"Captain, I'm sure my urine container has split open, my feet are squelching as I walk and it's a furnace inside my suit," Jackson moaned with a frustrated impatience.

"Might not be just your piss bag that's split open sunny," jeered Kovitz much to Jackson's horror, who hopped from one foot to the other to avoid treading in shit, only then realising his stupidity. The Guards, even the Captain, laughed.

The group gingerly padded down the ramp into darkness. They all put their suit lights on, giving off a white and cold artificial hue onto the stone walls as they proceeded deeper. After several minutes, they came to a dead end. Just a smooth wall blocking any further progress. That is when Carting noticed a fine line in the floor and the walls five metres from the end wall, "This could be some sort of lift. Look at those lines all around the tunnel."

Hadley inspected the lines and agreed, "Indeed, Carting, you are right. Now, the question is, how do we operate it?" everyone looked around for some sort of control panel, but with no success.

"Perhaps it's automatic," perked up Jackson.

Perez giving a once over on the situation agreed and told everyone to place themselves near the end wall and within the lines. When everyone was assembled, an unseen light in the stone ceiling came on and the lift shuddered and then went down.

"I guess we don't get to choose what floor we want, eh?" exclaimed Darby.

"It would appear so," said Hadley.

After a couple of minutes of slow decent, they arrived at the lower level, which opened up to a corridor leading off into darkness. No signs, no doors, just a square tunnel leading away.

"Well, when you only have one choice, why put up signs, eh?" noted Dellmayer.

"Ok all, let's go," ordered Perez, his light leading into the darkness. Fifty metres later, they came to the end of the corridor and onto a deep and large balcony with metal railings and stairs leading down on each side, "Dellmayer, get that spot light set up so we can at least see something."

"Yessir." A few moments later, he lit it up. They all gasped as an enormous cavern opened up to them, the end of which the lamp could not shine. There was a haze in the air, which hindered the view, but what they could see was purely wonderful. Below them were hundreds of statues of what seemed like stone. Each form was identical. Standing at three metres, they were like an aubergine stood up on end with an egg at the top. No other features were apparent. Lined up uniformly on the cavern's floor, they gave off an ominous aura, shadows playing with their imagination and, of course, their fear.

"Amazing!" exclaimed Hadley as he drew out a portable echo sounder.

"Somewhat discomforting," said Darby.

"No shit," added Draxler, "Gives me the fucking creeps."

"Ok guys, we'll go down one set of stairs together and remain within eyesight of each other. Is that understood everybody?"

Mumbles and yesses came back through the comms, "Ok, let's go."

As they were moving down the stone stairway, they all had that familiar sensation they experienced when approaching the Spike. It took much longer to go down than their minds would have thought so. Even counting the steps, they seemed to multiply the second you took an eye off them. Once they were down below, Hadley went straight up to the first statue and stroked it with his gloved hand, "It's warm. Carting, do you have that radiation counter out yet? We need to find out the levels we are dealing with here?"

"Doing it now," a few moments later, his device beeped and gave off a reading, "Radiation levels down here are much less than up top. I think the reactor, or whatever, is protected."

"And the air?"

"Give me a moment, I'll test it," Carting fumbled with a small sensor which he had drawn from a thigh pocket and started it up. A few moments later he exclaimed, "It seems fine; Oxygen and Nitrogen levels are like earth while the other gases vary within tolerable limits. There do not seem to be any toxins, but my device is by far not exhaustive. We should be able to breathe it though, especially with the radiation down to acceptable levels."

Hadley was the first to lift his visor. They all looked expectantly at him as he drew his first lungful. He smiled, "Seems fine, muggy and dusty, but certainly breathable." He took off his helmet and laid it on the floor at the bottom of the stairway. The others did the same.

"Thank god for that," Jackson said, taking in deep breaths with clear relief.

Dellmayer had left the lamp on the balcony shining over the expanse. They meandered for half an hour through the shadows and statues on a smooth shiny stone floor, before coming to the far end and halted before huge double-sided sliding doors. They rose five metres above them and eight metres wide, set back into the wall, covered in engraved writings nobody had a clue about, but all agreed to the beauty of the script or was it decoration. Swirls, geometric lines and some angular markings made a fresco set in stone to honour even the Egyptians.

"Truly alien in design. Gentlemen, we are within the walls of an ancient edifice built by a civilisation-,"

Draxler interrupted the Professor, "We've got company!"

Chapter 5

Trespassing

Perez swung around, rifle raised, and already scanning the area when he saw Draxler backing out of the shadows toward them, followed by a small plump humanoid. Draxler backed up fully into her group who now faced the singular alien who looked up to them with strange catlike eyes blinking wildly. Perez looked him over. He didn't seem to wear many clothes, a cloth around his midsection, but was totally naked otherwise. No gear, no attachments, nothing. He stood on two large trunk-like legs, each ending in a stubby foot with six claws arching out and digging into the ground. He had a stocky human body with long thin arms, which reached down to his knees. Perez saw the hands, a mix of two fat fingers and three large in-curving claws. A bone protrusion stuck out opposing his 'Fingers'.

Three red lasers were dancing on the alien's chest as Perez and his men stood in a rigid crouch. There was a silence for a moment and Perez wondered what to do now, "Hadley, your call," he managed through a voice wrought with incertitude.

Hadley took a step forward, evidently excited, and opened his arms in a gesture of peace and friendship.

"Hope you're not looking for a hug mate, hate those touchy feely moments," the alien said with an Australian accent.

Hadley, along with all the others, gasped, "You speak English?" Hadley managed after catching his breath.

"Duh, no, wotdayafink mate, double dutch?! Na, me speak English. Proper like," he said, walking around in a circle to the perplexity of the group. Draxler was moving to one side to get its flank, "Well, first things first. I would appreciate it if you would not mind lowering your guns. Wotdayafink? That I'm going to trample you to death? And you, lady, if you mind not trying to sneak up on me. Making me feel uneasy, it is."

Perez paused a second, then gave everyone a signal to lower their weapons.

"That's better," it said, notably relieved, "What is it with you lot, you come in here trespassing, chipping away at our Caster, damaging it probably, then go walking around 'ere like it was home. Come on, guys. Oh, and what's with the aggression. Guns!"

"Trespassing?" inquired Hadley.

"Well yeah, this is my place; I live 'ere. There is a doorbell ye know. Guess you missed it. I should move it to somewhere more visible. Anyway, my name is Ugar'philde. But you can call me Gar, if you like and no jokes about Garfield please, I know I am small but I haven't tasted pizza yet so no similarities. I am the guardian of this joint and have been for too long if you ask me."

Darby moved up front after having hid behind a stunned Dellmayer, "Eh Gar, you seem quite a cool guy. How come you speak English? Oh, I'm John, by the way."

"Watcha mate. Well, since this outpost is the nearest to your home, they gave me the eh esteemed privilege to study your planet, species and cultures," Gar paused for a second, "Yeah, it sucks, but it keeps me busy. Then I report every now and again to the Core about you and what yer all up to."

Hadley coughed as an introduction, "My name is Professor Hadley, pleased to meet you."

"You won't be for long mate, you remember me talking about trespassing. Well? What's it going to be? I like company, been too long I've been alone here, but there'll be all hell to pay when my boss gets a hold of this. He'll go ballistic! Being invaded by humans and all. Not on. And uninvited as well. Not going to go down well, my friends."

"What does that mean?" Perez interjected.

"My race are not all philosophizing intellectuals like me self."

"Yeah, right," snorted Dellmayer and Jackson at the same time.

"I'll have you know I am respected in the Core," Gar puffed his chest.

"Got it," Stone said, "That's why they sent you to this lost outpost in the middle of nowhere, alone?"

"It's not like that. This is a privilege... of sorts. Anyway, want a drink? Never spoken so much in so so many years, throat is dry as a dead lizard's asshole," Gar gave a smile that seemed awkward on his angular blue hewn face. "Come on, this way," he gestured by swinging one of his long arms in the air toward the side of the cavern. They all looked at each other and shrugged. Hadley was the first to follow Gar.

They arrived at the side of the cavern along which were several openings they hadn't seen before. They all followed Gar into an opening but he spun around and said, "Ok, you guys, foremost, you need to clean up. You're all stinking this place out," he said, looking directly at Jackson.

"How do we do that?" asked Dellmayer.

"Just strip off and make a pile on the ground. I'll get Mathilda to gather up your stuff and clean it. Won't take long," Gar said glibly.

"That will not happen," said Draxler, the only female in the group.

Gar stopped himself from entering the opening and turned back around and took a long, pensive look, "Ok, I get it. I'll get you some cloth to wrap yourself in. Just a sec," he dived into the opening and came out several moments later with a pile of cloth, "Sorry, don't have your sizes in stock. This will have to do. No way you're coming inside like that. You're all filthy."

They stripped out of their suits and overalls and made a sodden pile of festering cloth, sweat, shit and piss. Jackson did a dance to celebrate his freedom from his suit, even though he was stark naked. Indeed, his suit's waste bladders had opened and yellow brown sludge plastered the inside of his suit and permeated his overall.

"Ok, Dellmayer and Draxler, keep your weapons at the ready and backpacks available. Never lose sight of them. Dellmayer, radio to Kovitz and tell him we're staying a while and will call in at hour intervals."

"Yessir."

"Ok, done? Good, now go through that door," Gar said, pointing a claw to another opening a few metres down, "You can all have a shower and an ionising scrub. Oh, and it's a communal shower so no bashfulness, eh?" he said looking at Draxler.

She rolled her eyes and went straight for the showers, "Give me ten," she admonished to nobody and everybody. Not even Perez allowed himself a snort.

While they were waiting, Gar moved up to them. "You're kind of lanky, aren't you?" he said, eyeing them up and down, "Except you, Mister. What was your name?"

"Perez, Captain Perez. And stop eyeing me up. You gay or what?"

"It's the first time I've seen humans in the flesh. May I touch?"

Perez sent him a glare that froze Gar on the spot, "Ok, ok, touchy aren't we? Anyway, now go get your showers and come on in afterwards. I'm dying for a beer."

"Beer?" lighted up Dellmayer.

"Yeah, wadayafink? Some exotic bubbling blue space cocktail. Na, none of that shit for me. Beer, home brew mate," he winked and disappeared through the opening.

One after the other, they came in from their showers feeling a lot more human. Jackson was happy to be free from his suit, still taking in deep breaths of air to expunge his lungs, his subconscious still imagining the stench. They were in a spacious area with a thankfully high ceiling, although they had to crouch to get through the entrance. "Please, sit down," Gar gestured to the long wooden table decorated with the same carvings as the door they had seen earlier. Along both sides were benches, also in wood with carvings of similar nature. A contraption occupied Gar who stood in the corner near what they thought was the kitchen. He was pulling beers for everyone in long slender blue-tinted glasses. Once they were all seated, Gar, being at the head of the table sitting on a chair slightly higher than the benches, rose his glass and said 'cheers'. They did the same and gulped down the beer.

"Wow, this is good Gar. Well done, mate," Dellmayer said.

Perez, despite the shower and beer, wore a grim face full of thoughts and questions. Hadley was admiring the carvings while the others were just savouring the moment of pure relief.

"No sweat, mate. My pleasure," he smiled, enjoying the company, "Ye know the shit gonna hit the fan when they find out I've been drinking with humans. What the hell, what a blast."

Jackson looked up from his beer, "So how come you got the job of being guardian for this place? I mean, must be boring."

Gar, who still had human facial characteristics despite his alien aspect, looked embarrassed, "Well, it's a long story, but it was that or the stasis chambers. Got to choose. At home, I'm considered a rebel or terrorist, and still am, opposed to our regime who controls our society, with emphasis on control. A mix between your Stalin and Hitler. Well, that is my point of view. They gave me this option. I can't communicate to any other people other than my direct superior. Also, seeing clearly the mess terrorists are making of your world, killing innocents and creating strife, they thought it would be a good learning curve for me. The bets are on that nobody else knows I'm here."

"So you blew up women and children?" said Draxler steely.

"Nooo, wouldn't do that. That is their doing and laying the blame on us. I say us because we are quite a large faction at home. The Elites are trying to keep a cap on it, but it's not working. The more they squeeze, the more that comes out."

"So what are your people or race called?" Hadley said.

"The Xotle. But we are only part of many civilisations in the Galaxy. You being one of the less advanced. Probably due to you being so far out on a limb from the centre, or Core, as we call it, of the Galaxy. It's complicated and by far no paradise. Some civilisations are pure warmongers while others are more peaceful, dealing in trade rather than conquering," he stopped for a moment to consider the ceiling. They all look up but found nothing but stone, "Which makes a perfect transition to your situation. If some of those races get to know you've just gone galactic, so to say, they will come like hungry wolves to lost sheep. You being the sheep. But, on a happier note, there are benevolent societies that will offer to protect you. Depends on who gets to you first. That is out of my hands."

"We're in danger?" asked Hadley.

"Indeed, you are. Before, you had nothing of interest. Now that you're mobile, so to say, you'll be a threat or an annoyance."

Perez shifted uneasily on the bench, making it move for everyone on his side, "Do you have information or proof of what you say. Writings, pictures, videos that we can show our people. They won't believe us if we just say, gear up folks, shits coming."

"And some tech would be nice," added Darby, "You are obviously far more advanced than we are."

"Good point, Darby," said Hadley, "That Spike, for example, what is it and what is this place?"

"Oh, you mean the Caster, simple, it casts a portal through either time or space or both. Depends on how you set it. Our ships have them as well, well the military ones. Civil and commercial aren't allowed to have them. They have to go through the portals set up around the Galaxy and controlled by the Elite. Anyway, each military ship has a Caster set up on its nose to project a portal as and when necessary. Quite handy, really. More beers?" he smiled.

Yesses came around in a chorus of reprieve from the news they were receiving. Getting up to serve more beers, he said, "Your inertia drive is sensas! And that idea to grapple an asteroid up front to get mass and protect your ship is real cool. Of course, through the portal you won't need any of that, but in system travelling, would be an improvement on what we have despite all our so-called advance technology. You humans are quite ingenious, really. So philistine in how you treat each other and how the powers that be abuse the populace, treating them purely as money generating units, in a myopic race to get and keep ahead and above the others, yet you are so resourceful. No barriers when inventing stuff, and absolutely so courageous. The way you set off those nukes and flew into space like that. Really mad, but still fantastic at the same time. Something we don't have. With us, it's the status quo as always. 'Don't rock the boat, we're on a roll, change nothing' is their motto. Could be their demise as well if people like you get really going. You humans are a singularity, you have a true Alpha attitude like I've never seen in the Galaxy. I shudder at what you might be capable of. Which probably won't happen. Like I said, sheep to wolves and all."

"Well, that's cheery," said Draxler, sipping her fresh beer, "This is fantastic, Gar. How do you make it?"

"Oh, Mathilda flies out every now and again to the north to gather some grains of some sort. No idea what, but it works. I get the yeast from the Dates I grow here in the gardens. Lovely doubly."

"Who is Mathilda?" asked Perez, wary.

"Mathilda, lazy piece of junk if you ask me. No initiative, always powering down when you need her."

"I heard that Garfield," an artificially generated voice came from the entrance.

Gar looked up and snorted, "Don't call me Garfield. You know I hate it. I should stop showing you the vids from Earth."

"Well, I don't take kindly to you calling me lazy. I don't drink beer all day and sleep all night. And who has to clean up after you. And your guests, leaving a pile of shit for me to clean."

"It's not all glamour, darling. You knew it when you signed on," chided Gar.

"Don't call me darling. And my memory banks don't recall any signing on," she hissed.

"Sweetie pie, honey bunch, sugar plum…," he had to duck to avoid a chunk of stone deftly threw his way.

"Are we interrupting something, Gar?" smirked Dellmayer.

"So who or what is Mathilda?" Hadley asked again looking at her in the opening. Mathilda was obviously of the feminine nature but very short yet still having those curves in the right places and despite her metallic sheen, skin and green eyes, appeared quite attractive, even without hair.

"She's an android, a robot if you like. Nothing but a load of circuits and chips," Gar replied, stealing a glance at Mathilda, who came up to him slowly. Gar shrank back into his seat, "Just joking, luv. You know me," he chuckled.

"Yes, I do, and you know me better than that. Eh? What about the nights this pile of circuits spends keeping you comfy? Eh?" she stared at him. Her green luminous eyes drilling into him. Gar gave flitting, embarrassed looks around the table and an awkward silence fell onto the group. Someone snorted.

Thankfully for Gar, Dellmayer piped up, "Well, this is merry. What do you do for food here? I'm starving," giving a welcome distraction for everybody.

Grateful for the diversion, Gar jumped up and opened up a few cupboards, producing containers of some sort, "Just a sec, I'll heat this up. Leftovers from last night and some bread, ok?"

"Fine, I think. What is it?" asked Dellmayer.

"It's a meat Mathilda gets from her hunting missions. She's great at catching animals. The forest up North is full of them. And I added some vegetables and made a stew. Should be ok for you all. And the bread comes from the grain she gets as well. She's really handy around here."

"Don't overdo it, Garfield," Mathilda eyed everyone, then added, "Your suits and overalls are outside and clean. Help yourself." she went to leave. Dellmayer couldn't help looking at her backside as she sauntered out.

"Nice chick, like so many we have on Earth. So beautiful yet so…"

"That'll do, Dellmayer." Perez interrupted.

Hadley was fiddling with his plate like it was a specimen to dissect, then asked, "Gar, do you have any super powers? You know, like moving stuff or zapping things with your fingers?"

Gar threw a look at Mathilda, who was still in the entranceway, and was about to open his mouth when she spoke up with a chuckle, which was strange coming from her vocal mechanism, but she managed it well, "The only superpowers I've seen him have are when he cleans up his own mess instead of asking me and perhaps a few times during the night. So don't get overexcited."

Ignoring her, Gar said, "In fact, I have super powers but I prefer to keep them discreet ye know," he said, looking down at the table.

Somebody snorted and rolled their green mechanical eyes.

Having eaten and put on their overalls, leaving the suits for later when they had to leave, they followed Gar to the large doors they were at earlier, "I'll give you a brief tour. Won't hurt. I think," Gar said as he touched a remote that he had put on his wrist earlier. The doors slid open with a slow grinding movement, the stone upon stone making everyone cringe.

They all moved into a large open expanse filled with machines and terminals. "This is the control centre and where I communicate from. It's also where I get the feeds from Earth. At the back there, is one of our Casters." A long slender spike laid horizontally, the large end, attached to a large contraption made of shiny metal with a console fitted onto the side. "The Caster creates a portal against the wall to your right and through that I can send messages or receive them instantly from anywhere in the network normally, but they calibrated mine to one destination only. My boss's operation room. Like I said, they have muted me because of my...," he made air quotes, "Activities."

Hadley was of course running around everywhere looking at the different machines, not really knowing what they do, "The fusion reactor is behind those walls to your left. It provides the energy for this station and the Casters."

"Fusion?" said Hadley, "Why the radiation then?"

"Oh, that'll be defences," Gar said, not adding any more explanations.

"Oh, ok then, what is the big Caster on the surface for?"

"Well, for opening a portal in space, of course. Wadayafink it was, a work of art like your Eiffel Tower? They won't spend money on trivialities like that. This is all business. Anyway, the thing is, this one here," he said, gesturing toward the Caster in the room, "Is all set up to send messages and vid, automatically, so... my friends, they are certainly already aware of your presence here. I wouldn't hang around too long if I were you."

That gave thought to all. "What would they do if they came now?" a fretting Darby asked.

"Take you in, of course. They'll ask questions and so on then probably lock you away. I'm not too sure what would happen to your ship the Vanity. I don't know its defensive capabilities nor the manoeuvring skills of your pilot. At any rate, if they came in like now, you don't stand a chance in hell of getting away and your ship would get captured, if possible, if not, disintegrated."

They all stood in horror, realising the danger they were in, "Don't worry too much, knowing the operation department, they won't get their shit together before several hours if not days. They might not even come in. Hopefully, they will content themselves with my reports."

Perez suddenly stiffened, "Ok guys, we can't afford to hang around. Everyone in their suits and we leave now."

"But all this technology, it's so... out of this world. We could gain years in development by using only a small fraction of it. We can't leave now!" Hadley stamped his foot in a near tantrum as he finished his sentence.

"I for one would like to leave," said Jackson and Darby almost simultaneously. Hadley glared at them.

"Yeah, I guess we should skip off," Carting said.

"We're leaving, that's final," Perez glared at Hadley, "Dellmayer, get a message to Kovitz, tell him to get prepared for fast extraction and send him a recording of our conversation with Gar and to relay it to the Vanity. I mean the last bit of our conversation. Not that bit in the eh... kitchen. Get to it now.”

“Yessir.”

“Gar?” Hadley said, rubbing his chin, “Would it be workable to use your main Caster to leave if we had to quickly?”

“Yeah, mate, but I wouldn’t advise it. There are no receiving portals around Earth, so if I aimed you at your system, it’s pot luck if you don’t end up in the sun. Or worse, you could just get lost in space. Loved the film, not the series. Dr. Smith was cool. Anyway, not a good idea. Quantum mechanics is a bitch like that,” Gar paused, thinking deeply, “What I can do, is send you back in time. It does that as well...”

The sound of grinding of stone upon stone, but much louder than what the doors had made earlier, suddenly interrupted him, “What’s that?” exclaimed Draxler as she levelled her rifle along with Perez and Dellmayer.

“Oh shit, they did it the buggers,” Gar swore.

“Did what?” Perez asked impatiently.

"Activated the Sentinels," Gar said, like it was self-explanatory.

Chapter 6

Quantum entanglement and bunny rabbits

"And…," Perez insisted.

"They are the statues hanging around in the cavern. Quantum entangled, eh how did that film call them, Monsters of the Id? Yes, the Forbidden Planet, way ahead of his time the guy who wrote that. Anyway, once they get entangled with you, like looking at it will entangle you with them, they will become your worst nightmare. But it will be different for each one of you. For some it could be mild, for others, pure hell. Phobias you have; heights, spiders, sharks, tax bills etc and also any imaginative creatures like ghosts, demons, the mother-in-law or the like will become real and personified by those statues."

"How do you get around them? There are dozens of them!" ranted Jackson.

"But if they act upon our subconscious, why all the monsters? Can we not just think about bunny rabbits?" Hadley said hopefully.

"Indeed, you can, or try, but they play on the emotional state of the moment. It being fear, those horrors will surface. If you are not afraid and can think of bunny rabbits jumping around waiting for a cuddle, then good luck with that."

"Well, that's great," said Stone, looking back and forth with anxiety, "We need to get back to the shuttle! And that's the only way."

Hadley had edged up to look through the door into the cavern, and he let out a gasp of horror and ran straight back to cower behind the others, "It's full of Spiders, giant stone Spiders with mandibles and legs and things. It's horrific. I can't go," upon that, no one could help but to peek around through the doors. They all let out shrieks and gasps of pure fear.

"What did you see?" Hadley said to the group. They all answered with different versions of their own phobias, some giant crabs with pincers, others, demon-like ghosts, flames of fire or looked into a never-ending abyss which could engulf them into eternity.

"Like I said, not good," added Gar after they had nearly all gave their own version of fear. He looked at Hadley, who had simply lost it. Jackson was peeing in his overall and Darby, although stoic, was coming out in a feverish sweat dripping from his brows, "You're quiet, Stone, what's your fear?" said Gar casually.

He looked around the others hesitantly and said, "Not being good enough," he finally said weakly.

Everyone looked at him. But Gar continued, "And how does that pan out with the Sentinels, Stone?"

"This may sound stupid, but my wife and our son…," he looked down to the floor, lost in his memories. A silence invaded the room except for the continued shuffling of stone upon stone from outside.

Dellmayer broke the silence, "Can't be that bad mate, me and my Giant Spiders an all, we could do a deal. No? I have a way with women."

Draxler snorted.

"It's not like that. It was my fault, I was stupid and… they died…," he cried, "They were both looking at me, blaming me for their deaths. They have been haunting me for years now. I didn't think they would come back to kill me. I am so sorry. I am so sorry," he sobbed.

Draxler came up to him and put a hand on his shoulder. She said in a soft tone, "What did you do that was so stupid, Stone?"

"We were living in Virginia, Greensboro, and I booked them a flight to Seattle for a break. It was tense at home. I was always away, what with the training and all, distracted. I should have gone with them, but let them go. I let them go to their deaths."

"What do you mean, Seattle's not that bad," said Dellmayer.

"Their plane crashed on final approach. I should have spent more time with them, they wouldn't have left otherwise. We would still be together. It was all my fault. I messed up, and they died. I was a traitor to my family," he looked up with bloodshot, teary eyes, "Don't you see man, I killed my family! And now they're back… in there, waiting for me," he collapsed on the ground, a mound of shuddering tears and crying sobs.

Looking at the group, Gar spoke up, "Well, on a merrier note, I have a solution, but you will not like it."

"I think anything will do the job, Gar," said Perez, looking down at Stone and then toward the others.

"Sir?"

"Yes, what is it, Dellmayer?" answered Perez.

"Kovitz has had contact with the Vanity. They are reporting sightings of three vessels in the system. Captain Derrick wants us back immediately."

"They're here already? Shit," started Gar, "Gonna go down badly."

"Tell him we're on our way, Dellmayer," he turned grimly to Gar, "Ok Gar, what was your solution?"

Gar hopped around nervously from one foot to the other, "Well, I can open the planetary Caster and get your ship to safety in the past. I wouldn't risk sending them anywhere, too hazardous, but a short trip into the past should put them in safety. Then they can leave. The other ships won't know how far back I'd sent them. They would have to come here and consult the parameters I'd set up. By then the Vanity could skedaddle."

"Good, seems like a solution for them. What about us, we have that cavern to go through, you know? Not a walk in the park. We need to get to the shuttle and join the Vanity before they leave," Perez said, thinking over the dire situation.

"Well, that's the part you will not like. Instead of going through the cavern, you go through this Caster," Gar said hesitantly, waving his long arm toward the horizontal Caster at the back of the room.

Hadley, having gathered his senses, heard the idea, "But you said it will go to one place only, your operations centre back home."

"Well, that's the part I thought you might not like. Either you risk the cavern or you go through to my home world."

Perez, feeling a welling frustration, said, "And what do you think they would do to us? Kill us? Imprison us?"

"Hard to say mate, they could invite you for a meal and a chat or blast you with ray guns! No idea," Gar inspected his claws, trying to look detached.

"Well fucking great, either-or eh?" said Draxler furious.

"This could be a marvellous opportunity to introduce humans to the others. We would be ambassadors, ambassadors to the stars! They would surely be glad to meet us," Hadley said perking up at the idea.

Gar snorted, "Yeah, right, like ye mother-in-law would buy you a Rolex. They're up to their ears in racial conflict. Another civilisation on the chessboard won't go down well, I am sure. But you never know. It's a fair chance. Probably better than to go through there," he finished pointing through the doors.

"Well, I for one would like to take that risk. The chance is too enticing to pass off," Hadely said, looking at Jackson, Darby and Carting.

"While I abhor taking unquantifiable risks, I think I'll come with you Professor," said Darby, a wan smile showing on this thin lips.

"Jackson?" Hadley asked.

"I'm in. We could learn so much."

"Indeed, Jackson. Good," Hadley rubbed his hands and turned to Carting.

"I'll risk going through the cavern. My phobia is... eh controllable...," he said, not with a little fear in his voice.

"Anyone else for the Galaxy ride?" said Gar.

Both Dellmayer and Draxler looked at Perez, who said, "This is your call guys. No orders. I'm going through the cavern. Kovitz is alone," he looked heavily at Stone, who by now had got up and gathered his wits, "We need a pilot. If you don't want to come, I won't insist. We can get the Vanity to send down another shuttle, but if you come with me, it would save us time, which I believe we have little of."

Stone threw a look at the large opening leading into the cavern, "I'll come with you," then stared at the ground, lost within himself.

"I'll stay Captain, it's my job anyway and to hell with giant spiders," said Dellmayer casually hefting his rifle.

Perez nodded to him and looked at Draxler.

"I'll come too," she said without further words, but looking at Carting.

Perez's look shifted from Draxler to Carting, then back to Draxler. He wanted to ask something but thought better of it, "Very well. Excellent."

"Right, let me set this all up then. One portal for Vanity's escape, let's say, one month in the past, I'll put a two-hour timer on it. That should do. Even if my people come down here, it will be too late to read the setting. After two hours, it will delete. They won't be able to follow. And, of course, one portal for home. Coming up!" he said as he set the controls. They could all feel the energy released into the two Casters, making a further rumbling sound besides the grinding rocks in the Cavern.

Gar didn't see that Draxler had moved up behind him while he was setting the controls, nor the keen interest gleaming in her eyes. Nor when she went back to the controls when he had left.

"What about you, Gar?" Hadley said.

"Don't know, really. If I stay here, I am safe. Those rocks won't attack me. But there'll be hell to pay when my superiors come in. They'll ship me off to some oubliette somewhere lost in space. If I go back to my world, same story. But… if I can come with you guys?" he said looking at Perez, Stone and Draxler with wide oval eyes, "That would be snazzy. I get to be free at last and out of this hole."

Perez went up to Gar and looked down at him, "That is courageous of you, little one. I cannot guarantee you a smooth ride and what my people would think of you, nor what they would want to do. But it would serve as irrevocable proof of what we've discovered. You are welcome to come with us, Gar. You are brave."

"Aw brave dunno, self preservation really. And thanks," rubbing his hands gleefully, "Let's get this show on the road, happy campers!" he turned to his console, "Hadley, the Caster is ready when you are," he said, looking at Hadley and his team who had gathered together, "Good luck and say hi to Grath'Un from me. He's my 'keeper' let's say. He's ok, sometimes. Sometimes not. Depends on what day you catch him on. I would suppose today is not ideal. But there's a heart there somewhere."

Hadley and the others stood there hesitantly, "What do we have to do now?" he said looking at the portal which had opened up on the far wall, a shimmering blue infinity haze dying off into a black centre.

"You just walk through. Easy peesy."

They all said their goodbyes and slaps on the shoulders, then set themselves before the portal, "Ok, here goes. Good luck to you all, friends," Hadley waved and then walked through the portal. The other two followed with grim looks, but not without heightened anticipation. When they left, Gar turned the device off, leaving a silence in the room save for the distant grinding of stone and the constant humming of the main Caster.

Chapter 7

Quantum untangled

"Right let's get this done, shall we? Any suggestions?" Perez asked to no one in particular.

"We go barging through on a run," gave Dellmayer, not feeling it at all.

"Draxler?"

"No idea, snakes, they are long and all over the place. Not sure there would be many gaps," she said, gritting her teeth.

"Whatever suits you all. I think any which way is bad," rumbled Carting moving toward Draxler.

"Stone?"

"Eh no idea, perhaps going around the side. That way we could duck into one of those openings, if needs be."

"Good idea, Stone. Gar, any ideas?"

"Well, in fact Stone is right, it is best to go along the side. But along with that I would suggest something else," Gar said reservedly.

"And…?" Perez said impatiently.

"In view that I am immune to their attacks, that I lead you while you all put your hands on each other shoulders, with your eyes closed. Bit like a queue leu, ye know, ye get at weddings and stuff like that," Gar scratched his bald head.

"Why would closing our eyes be a good idea?" Dellmayer asked.

"They are quantum machines feeding off your fears and like quantum mechanics only come into action if you look at them, you would become entangled with them. Being blind would calm your fears, and their power would be less. If you faced them straight on, it would be suicide. Your fears would begat more and more action from them. Zen attitude and all that shit, that's the way to go, ye know."

"Ok, so we walk through a cavern of monsters, blind and following you in a snake dance, and that's going to get us through?" Perez snorted.

"Well, sort of. If anyone opens their eyes, their fears will only multiply and from then on in it will only be an escalation of destruction. That's how the theory goes, anyway. Quite ingenious, if you ask me."

"Hmm, right. Ok, you lead, then Dellmayer, Draxler, Stone and Carting, I'll take the rear. This is going to be fun," said Perez, not believing a single word.

They all got in line, then advanced to the wide-open doors to the cavern, "Remember to keep your eyes closed and pray, if you like. Think of pleasant things, which might help. Oh, and we have to stop at the kitchen area to pick up your suits, remember. The suits belonging to Hadley and others can be left behind, they will only hinder your progress. I'll call Mathilda to meet us at the lift. She'll want to come as well, maybe."

Dellmayer stooped to put his hands on Gar's small shoulders, and everybody followed suit. They entered the cavern and turned left, following the wall. The stone forms immediately approached them, but none could frighten or touch the group. After they had moved about one hundred metres along the side of the cavern, Stone opened his eyes to a nearby grinding of stone that he felt touch him. It was a mistake. Suddenly, his wife and son came at him shouting obscenities and blame, to which Jack screamed, "No! I'm sorry, so sorry, don't!" His wife got in a downward swipe with her stone hand. He dodged with his body but was too late to pull his leg away. The crunching sound of his leg snapping at the tibia made him scream, which alerted Draxler to open her eyes, bringing on a pile of giant snakes. Dellmayer, not able to remain inert, opened fire on several approaching Spiders, leaving glowing blast marks on their legs and bodies but having little or no effect neither to the horrific clucking sound they gave out nor to them advancing.

"Close your eyes everybody!" shouted Gar over the din of grinding stone and pulses, "We've arrived at the kitchen." Perez had fired as well, but the general panic made everyone run past Gar in stark white fear. Perez scooped up Stone and carried him through the entrance, following the others. Once they were in safely, everyone panting and eyes wide with terror, Gar stood in front of them like a teacher telling children off in a classroom, "Well fantastic, smart, you supposed to be crack commandos and Earth's finest and you run like kittens." He still gave them reassuring pats on their backs, "I know it's hard, but keep those eyes shut. Got it, everyone?"

Mumbles came through the panting, "Sorry, I started it." Stone said, "Something brushed my side, and I automatically opened my eyes."

Draxler glared at him, "Well, next time try not to scream like a baby, eh?"

"That looks bad," said Perez grimly, looking at Stone's broken tibia, "I must carry you the rest of the way. We can get that fixed in the shuttle."

"I didn't open my eyes until we had to run, but it was horrible. Those flames were real, I felt the heat lashing out at me," said Carting with a tremble.

"Well, at least you see what we are up against. Anyway, we made progress. Ok guys, suit up and let's go. Perez, can someone help Stone into his suit?" Gar said, trying to encourage them with a light modulation in his voice. He glanced at Stone, "Hold on, mate, not far now."

Once everyone suited, Dellmayer spat on the floor, then put his hands on Gar again, "Ok let's do this."

This time everyone, through fear of facing their worst nightmares or pure panic, kept their eyes closed and hugged the wall as they made their way to the end. Stone had an arm on Draxler's shoulder in front while he was being carried by Perez, the jogging making him scream in pain at each jolting footfall.

"Ok guys, keep your eyes shut, we're at the bottom of the stairs. You must pick up your helmets then run like a rabbit up the stairs... Now GO!" A pandemonium of rushing feet and grabbing hands later they were all racing, for the love of their lives, up the stairs. Once at the top Gar put a hand on Mathilda who was waiting for them and said, "Well done, you limeys, you did it! We're safe now. The Sentinels can't exit the cavern. Well, not according to the instruction leaflet I got. Let's go."

Relieved, they all avoided even a glance back into the cavern. Only the dark and faceless corridor found their captivated interest. Once on the lift they all put their helmets on, relieved to hide the pure fear still haunting their faces from each other. When the lift came up they all ran out and up the ramp with Dellmayer half carrying Stone, to find open air and sky, a welcome sight after having spent but only a few hours in the oppressive underground base.

Kovitz came up to them with a slight jog, "Thank god your all back safe," then he jumped back and raised his rifle at Gar, "What's that? And where are the lab guys?" he shouted.

Gar rolled his eyes, "Captain, are all your men gun happy when they see something new?"

Perez moved up to stand between Kovitz and Gar, "It's alright Kovitz, he's a friend and that eh woman next to him is an android, friendly. We met them down there. Gar, that's his name, was the guardian of this place."

"Was?" Kovitz asked.

"Well, it's complicated, but he's coming with us, and the others… they're ok but we'll explain later. Let's get going, we have little time. What's the situation upstairs Kovitz?"

"Grim, Sir, the last message I had was twenty minutes ago. They were attacked and took some damage. The last report confirmed one ship approaching, maybe a boarding party. I've been trying to contact them since, but nothing. But the

Vanity is still there. I'm still getting their transponder signal."

"Ok everybody, into the shuttle. We have little time before that portal closes and we still must get past their ships. We've got to get that leg fixed Stone and some painkillers into you. Do you think you'll be able to pilot that thing?"

"I'll try, depends on the painkillers."

"That's the spirit, ok let's go." They all piled into the spacious shuttle, made to accommodate fifteen people with seating. It had sanitary amenities and a good stock of dehydrated food, recycled air and a good supply of water, it too recycled. It would have to do for the journey home, if they could not make the Vanity and had to go through the portal.

Chapter 8

The Portal

An hour later they were in space and heading for the portal. Gar giving a few comments about how snazzy the inertia drive was. 'Tugless' he said while patting the hand of Mathilda who was sitting next to him, taking it all in like it was an audit of accounts. The shuttle's sensors could track the other ships and the Vanity but they did their best to avoid being detected by going around the long way over the horizon and coming up on the opposite side of the portal. Gar had said that they could go through on either side. Stone, meanwhile, had had his leg set and held in place by a plasti-clasp and high on painkillers.

"They've got her all right. Those three vessels surround the Vanity. Can we make it to the portal before they notice us, Stone?" Perez asked.

"We're coming up to the portal at a good speed. If they notice us now, it will already be too late, unless they use a ray-gun on us," as he said that, a ray of light swished through the port side of the shuttle, blackening the windows on that side, but no apparent damage had occurred. "Wooh! That was close. Taking evasive action, hold tight everyone!" Stone said as he adopted a corkscrew movement through space in ever-increasing circles, dodging several blasts. They were almost impossible to hit with a direct shot.

"This is fun!" exclaimed Gar as the swirling shuttle made almost everyone else want to vomit. Before everyone realised, they had pierced the blue/black field of the portal and were on the other side. A calm passed over for a few moments as Stone checked his sensors, "We're in the clear. There is nothing around us except the planet. Oh, and we had thirty seconds left to make it through, otherwise it would have closed on us!"

Everyone gave out a sigh of relief as Stone levelled the shuttle out on a regular plane.

"Fucking brill mate," said Gar to Stone, "You're one of the best."

"Yeah, thanks Stone, you did it!" Kovitz said, clearly relieved.

"I wonder what will happen to the Vanity and the crew?" said Carting to no one in particular.

Gar jumped up from his seat to look out of a clear window, "They'll take them back to the core. What they do to them, I don't know. Nor what will happen to Hadley and his people either. But for now everyone is safe at least."

"Ok, first things first. We need to grab an asteroid to give us mass. Gar, is there an asteroid field in this system?" Perez turned to him.

"Yep, just after the third planet and hang a left, can't miss it."

"Got it," said Stone as he entered some coordinates on his systems sensor's maps and directed the ship to follow the course, "It'll take a few hours, I guess."

Clapping his hands, Gar gleamed, "I'm dying to find out what you have for grub!"

Draxler chuckled, "Don't get your hopes up too much, it's about as bland as a grain of sand in the desert."

"How long will it take to get to Earth?" asked Gar, rummaging through the cupboards at the back of the shuttle.

"Depends on the size of the asteroid we get, the bigger the better and the quicker. But we're talking about several months."

Gar stopped rummaging, "What, we have to put up with this for months on end. We'll go mad."

Mathilda clicked her eye open, "Won't change much for you. I might just shut off though, I can feel some good energy in the ship's generator. I'll be fine, thank you."

Gar snorted, "Yeah, always out for ye self, darling. Where's the beer?"

"It's going to be a long ride, I can feel it," said Draxler, looking at Carting who had moved up beside her.

"You two want a room?" joked Gar.

"Shut up!"

"So, we're a month back in time, is that right Gar?" said Perez.

"Yep."

"Good, won't make any difference to them back on earth," he replied with relief.

"Eh Sir, that's not quite true," said Draxler, looking nervously at Carting.

"What does that mean?" said Kovitz, "What's not quite true?"

Perez looked up from a tablet and stared at Draxler, waiting for a reply.

"Well, when Gar set the time scale to one month. I, eh, changed it," she said hesitantly.

"What!" blasted Gar, "You dabbled with my controls? You could've made so many mistakes just by looking at them. What did you do?"

Everyone was looking intently at Draxler, which seemed to include Carting somehow. "Forty years in the past," she said sheepishly.

"Forty years!! Are you mad? Why did you do that?" Perez fumed. The others gave out gasps and gulps as the realisation of what she'd done set in. They would arrive on Earth not knowing anyone.

"Fucking bitch!" shouted Kovitz as he got up and dashed toward Draxler. Perez got in-between them and pushed Kovitz back into his seat.

"Calm down, everyone," Perez caught his breath, "Now how do we deal with this?" Perez said, glaring at Draxler, "You could've asked first, you know. This concerns us all."

"Think of the advantages, everybody. We get to be the pioneers coming to earth from the future with advanced Technology. Deals with the government and the corporations. We'd all be rich," defended Carting looking at Draxler.

"Fuck you mate, you don't get to decide things like that," Kovitz was about to get up again when Perez held up a hand glaring at him.

"Gar?" Perez said, looking at the small alien who had joined the group, "What's going to happen? I mean, we will eventually meet ourselves," everybody's eyes locked onto Gar who felt suddenly tiny.

"Doesn't work like that. If you go back, you go back to an existence where you don't exist. It's a different plane of existence. No worries."

"No worries!" blurted Dellmayer uncharacteristically.

"Plus, it will give us time to prepare for… you know… them, the aliens," Draxler hastily added in a forlorn hope to placate their anger.

"The Xotle," Carting added.

"And what about our families and friends we left behind when we came out here? What would they think?" Stone said.

"Lost in space," feeling the tension in the air, Gar held back a crack about the film, "Look at it this way, you'll get to make amends and start over. Draxler messed up big time, but what is done, is done. We must make do. Mathilda here will be the sensation, though. Space android and all."

Mathilda huffed, "They try to take me apart I'll go nuclear on them!"

"You can do that?" asked Dellmayer, eyes wide.

"Yes, and many other nasty things, so no messing around with my circuits," her eyes flicked red for a few nanoseconds before resuming their normal green tint.

They all looked at Gar for confirmation, who nodded solemnly in return. A restless calm settled in, everyone lost in his or her own personal thoughts about those implications.

Several hours later, they came to the asteroid belt and chose the largest their shuttle's grips could handle. Once secure, Stone imputed the melody for the return journey and after several manipulations pressed a final command button, sending the ship earthwards. The shuttle slowly gathered speed, which would only level out at many times the speed of light. It would adopt the imputed trajectory by synchronizing the melody through the inertia device.

The Alpha Centauri system shrunk in their vid feeds, as the shuttle sped forward to an unsuspecting and, more so, unprepared Earth.

To be continued…

Albia

Mike Lees

I am not afraid… I was born to do this.

Jean d'Arc

Chapter 1

Albia

An April wind blew clean skies across the green lush meadow as Albia looked on with broken eyes. An oak tree and a felled log, her throne, and a vista of grand yet empty countryside, her realm. She wondered who she was? Sometimes, sitting alone here at her favourite spot just outside of York, a break from the turmoil and duplicity of modern life, she felt… otherworldly. Yes, that was the word, otherworldly. Where did she come from? Who was she? She laid down her half-eaten tuna sandwich and rested her red laden head into her palms, blotting out the view and seeking her inner self. No distractions, no interruptions, just her and nature, Mother Nature. Good, yet missing something. What made her different? She didn't mix with her school friends, feeling off in a blind society, led by blind guides, heading into oblivion, a wasteland of distress and futility. Yet, there was something, something for her, a destiny?

She shook her head. Red, long curls flowing with the movement, enhanced in the wind, glistening gold and copper, lighting up a contrast with the browns and greens of the countryside. She looked down the valley, a solitary farmhouse in the distance, smoke bellowing out of its chimney. A peaceful vista to calm her nerves.

She was a loner. No doubt about it. Ask her school friends. Well, school acquaintances would be more accurate. She was on a different plane, no mutual interests, no chemical bonding, and no boys!

She frowned.

Her last year at school, then what, college? Further education? To become attractive to a future Master? True, her parents would support her. They were well off and kind, but what to study when nothing drew your attention? The bland and bleak world coalesced in her mind. She'd spent hours in this spot, a refuge from the hustling and pretending of society. An allergy, bleeding sores into her heart, fighting her lust for more than the world could offer. Where did she get this sensation? Not her parents, a model of modern success, wealthy and prominent. It meant nothing to her.

Meaning. She desired meaning, needed it, to sail upon waters of her heart, to float upon clouds of love and walk upon lands of hope.

She looked up to the sky, saw the sun nearing the earth and thought it was between five and a quarter past, knew it even. No need for her watch or cell phone. She left them at home. No need anyhow. Chains to enslave. Here, before her Kingdom, she enjoyed freedom and was at one with her surroundings.

She huffed and got up to walk back home, an hour's trip. Good, still time to be with me and the emerald. She thought. She rose and stretched, arms out, lungs open to the clear air filling her body. As she exhaled, an acorn fell from the tree, hitting her shoulder and bouncing onto the log. She smarted at the surprise and saw the acorn settle finally onto the earth. Hm, Mother, you wish me to stay and admire your beauty still? She mused. She bent down to pick the acorn up, as one would open a letterbox to take a letter.

It felt heavy in her delicate hands and smooth beyond normal. She turned it around in her hand and noticed faint marks going around it. Or was it the waning light through the branches? No, it was marked. Not natural, embedded in the acorn. She held it up to the light. Indeed, some sort of inscription, yet unrecognizable. Now how could that be? An acorn falling from a tree with a sign on it... She looked up. The tree smiled back, waving its branches. She felt dizzy and sat down again.

How strange yet marvellous. A message for her! She gleamed in exquisite joy and glanced up at the Oak tree again. It bowed and breathed, a pleasant sound of rustling and swishing. Albia was ecstatic. Clasping the acorn in her small hand, she ran home across the dales and toward her destiny.

Chapter 2

The Missive

"Mum, look what I found, or rather it found me," Albia said, presenting the acorn to her mother once she had gotten home.

Her mother looked at it with mild interest, but when she saw the inscriptions, she let out a shudder, penetrating her entire body. She eyed her daughter with stern yet sad eyes.

"What's the matter mum?"

"Where or how did you get this, dear?"

"Eh, I was up by the meadows, you know, I always go there to be alone a while. This acorn fell from the tree I was under."

"Darling, you are always alone. Doesn't matter anymore."

"What do you mean by that?"

Her mother hesitated a second, "Do you know what this inscription says? It's quite small."

"No idea. Perhaps Dad can read it?"

"He can, dear. It's in Norse, ancient rune language. Wait for him to come home and he'll translate for you."

"You look worried, what's the matter," asked Albia to her wrought mother.

"It's just earlier than we thought. You are only sixteen, my love. Too young for this, for sure."

Albia squinted at her mother, suspicious and defensive, "Stop talking in riddles. What is this about? You seem to know something I don't."

"Well, at your birth, when I came home from the hospital we had a visit. An old man rang and said he had some information regarding you. We were sceptic, but your father let him in. He said that you were special. Nature's gift to the world. His name was Alfred. He said he was from the north. He had a really strong accent."

"Why didn't you tell me this before?" said Albia.

"We thought nothing of it. But he looked at you, as a baby, in reverence. Worried, I asked him to leave, but your father heard him out. You will get a calling when the time is right. How, he did not know. He called you Albia. A pleasant name that we adopted for you. He said it is a name of an ancient Pict Princess, also, that when you get the calling, we should support you in a quest. I suppose this is it," she said, looking at the acorn again. A sad look on her face.

Bewildered, Albia went upstairs to her room. This revelation was hard on her, so much yet so little information. It was frustrating. She, a simple girl from York, a loner for sure and thirsty for meaning in life. Ok, but a calling? A Pict Princess? She smiled. It answered so many questions she had flitting around in her head. The emptiness of her life, thoughts of not belonging to this world. One step ahead, or behind, never in phase, never the perfect teenager. She had to admit to herself, it all fit into place. A fantastic story though, hard to believe. She waited for her father to come home and translate the message. In the meantime, she opened up her laptop and did some research: Who were the Picts? Albia? Who was she? And why a calling? What could she do? So many unanswered questions dwelling in the forefront of her thoughts, kidnapping her reason and hijacking her subconscious, her soul.

She passed the time by brushing her wonderful red hair. A daily chore, but today she took her time, untangling what the whispering wind had messed up. She then gently brushed it, slowly and purposefully, like a caring mother to her child. As she progressed she felt more and more at ease, at peace with herself and confident that this calling, whatever that meant, would be positive. She finished her hair and plucked the brush clean with a comb and placed it back on the commode. A mirror was facing her. She caught a glimpse, surprised to see that her hair was so beautiful, regal even. Something she had not lingered on before. It was always a chore to brush her hair. Now… she felt like a Princess! She smiled with joy at her image, who smiled back with a wink. Startled, she got up and strode around her room, not daring to look in the mirror again. What was happening? She went to the window and drew back the net curtains to ponder the garden. As she looked, it was as though all the early spring flowers bent toward her, bowing. Even the boring Privet bushes bustled with life. The birch tree at the end seemed to twist around its trunk to face her, its young bright green leaves bristling in the dusk, celebrating. Albia looked on in shock. This wasn't a figment of her imagination, it was real. She looked over to the other gardens and saw sad stretches of starved lawns and sad bushes. When she looked back to her garden, everything was vibrant, gleaming in joy. A vista of celebration.

"What do you know I don't?" she asked the garden.

Bright colours suddenly erupting in the dim light was their answer. She stepped back from the window, flustered, unfamiliar yet bemused at all the attention. She smiled, curtsied and left her bedroom to glide down the stairs, feeling every bit like a Princess. When she got to the bottom of the stairs, she felt stupid. A Princess, yeah, right. She traipsed into the kitchen and got a soda from the fridge. Her mother was busy making the evening meal when she heard the door key turn and flew to the front door to greet her father.

"Hello dear, what's all the flustering about? You look excited about something." Then a shadow fell over his face, questioning. "Don't tell me, you have a boyfriend," he ventured like so many fathers, protective of their daughter.

"No, silly, you know me. No, it's this." She held out the acorn. By this time her mother came through and all three were standing in the hallway. Her mother shot a powerful glance at her father. Puzzled, he took it and beamed in delight at seeing the inscriptions laid around the acorn.

"Where did you get this?"

"It fell on me, from a tree when I was up at the meadows this afternoon. What does it say?" she asked.

"It looks like a version of ancient Norse. I'll have to look it up. But can I come home first? Give me a few minutes and I'll get what you want."

After a few tense moments waiting in the living room, her father came in and made for the large bookshelf, taking out a book without even looking at the title. He knew what he wanted. "Let me see, I have a book here which should be able to translate it. Norse is well known today and should not be a problem," he said as he sat down in his favourite armchair. "Can you get me a pen and some paper love? I'll have to write it down."

Albia ran into the kitchen and got them from a drawer and flew back into the living room. "Here you are." She was dancing on her toes for several minutes while her father translated the writing. Then, with a flourish, he ripped the paper off the pad and handed it to her.

She grabbed it and read: Ring of Brodgar, aloud. "What does that mean?" she added, looking at her father.

"It's an ancient site in the Orkneys. A ring of stones. Said to be built by the Picts millennia before Christ, when they first settled in these isles. The Orkneys are bristling with vestiges of their settlements and places of worship. Fascinating."

"What has that got to do with me? And on an acorn?" Albia said confused.

Her mother came into the room, "Jonathan, I have already told her about that man who came when she was born."

"Oh, I see. Well, this man was adamant that you were or are a Pict Princess, that's why we gave you your name. Albia is the name of a Princess from that time. We thought it was pretty and suiting. So we chose it. He said you would have a calling. I suppose this is it," he finished.

"And..." Albia crossed her arms.

"It would appear the old man was right. You're wanted at the Ring of Brodgar," he said, as if it was the most natural thing in the world.

"But what does this all mean? A calling, a Princess, the Picts, acorns with writing on them? What am I to all that?"

"Frankly darling, I don't know. But we'll have to find out. Or rather, you will. I can't leave work now. You know April is always the closing of yearly accounts and the deadline is imminent. I can't leave now. Either you wait and I'll go with you this summer or…" he trailed off.

"I can't wait for summer, Dad! This is too exciting… Or…, you said."

"Or," he cringed, "Jason."

"Jason! How can he help me?"

"Jason is twenty, drives a car, and is a very practical guy. You saw how he helped me last year with the garage doors. He knows a lot of stuff, useful stuff. And he's gay," he added, looking at his wife.

"What does that mean, 'he's gay'?"

"Darling, you are young, too young to go on your own, and Jason, well being gay, won't be a source of worry for us," he looked up to a frowning Albia.

Albia narrowed her eyes, "Don't you trust me or something?"

"It not you, its Jason we need to trust, and I do. He's a good lad and I am sure he will accompany you on your eh… quest."

"Dinner will be ready in ten minutes," her mother said gruffly.

Albia spent the evening and a good part of the night boning up on the Picts, their history and origins. Well, she was their Princess. Wasn't she? She was glad to have the many books from her father who had kept quite an extensive collection on the subject.

Chapter 3

The Princess's Paladin

Jonathan called Jason the next morning. It was Saturday and agreed he come to their place at two the same afternoon.

The bell rang at one fifty. "Hello Jason, come on in and thank you for coming around."

"No problem, what's up? That boiler pump playing up again?" said Jason as he entered the hallway.

"No, nothing as trivial as that. It something much more important. Please come into the living room."

Albia came down the stairs while Samantha came in from the kitchen. Once they were all settled down, Jonathan spoke, "Jason, Albia has received a message and needs to go to the Orkneys for a few days. We cannot accompany her ourselves, what with work and other commitments," he glanced at Samantha, "And we wondered if you would go with her, I mean drive her up there."

"Yeah, why not? I've got nothing to do at the moment. Out of work, you see. Yes, I'll be glad to go with her," he turned to Albia, "If you're ok with that?"

Albia frowned, "It's my Dad's idea. I guess it has to be."

Jonathan said to lighten the air, "Albia has received a message to go to the Ring of Brodgar."

"Oh, ok. What kind of message? Are we not going to see someone?"

Everyone looked at each other, then Albia said, "Go ahead Dad, it's your idea."

"Eh, well ok," he told Jason all that they knew about the old man who had visited, the message, and that Albia may be an heir to Princess Albia of the Picts. He then turned to Albia, "Can you show him the acorn?"

"Acorn?" said Jason.

Albia showed him the message written on the acorn and told him the meaning, "That's all we have for the time being. I need you to come with me and help me if you can," she finished staring him in the eyes.

Jason hesitated in the face of Albia's determination then said, "Ye ok, but I'm broke," he finished looking at Jonathan.

"Don't worry about that, Jason. I'll look after everything. You can even take our second car, much more reliable than your old Ford."

"Jonathan! I need that car. How can I go into town without it?"

"Dear, she'll only be gone a few days and frankly, your trips into town are hardly what I call a need. Think of it as you are giving your daughter support in such a strange situation. You know she needs to go?"

Samantha huffed and went back into the kitchen.

Jason's eyes went from Albia to her father's, not knowing what to say in such an awkward situation and preferring, wisely, to keep shut.

"Don't worry, she'll get over it. Thank you, Jason, for accepting. Albia, I'll contact school on Monday with a suitable explanation for your absence. In the meantime, we can make plans, the ferry to the island and lodgings. Get together some suitable clothes, it's probably awful up there and…" he said turning to Jason, "get together any tools or such that you might need. I had a look earlier on internet. The site seems quite accessible."

"Yeah, I guess. What a smash, eh Albia? You and me on an adventure!" he said, lightly punching her shoulder.

Albia sighed, "Right, a real wheeze!"

Chapter 4

The Princess rides

They made plans and set off on Monday at nine o'clock. The drive to Aberdeen would take six hours and then a six-hour ferry trip to Kirkwall, the principal town on the Orkneys.

"Your mother was tense when we left. Why would she be worried? We're just going for a trip to Orkney. Not like we're going around the world," Jason said as he drove the Kia up the A90.

"Well, you know mums, the always fuss. We have everything we need, good clothes, food and your bag of stuff, whatever you have in it."

Well, I suppose it's not every day somebody's girl goes on a witch hunt."

"It's not a Witch hunt, Jason," she cried.

"Ok, what is it?"

"Don't know."

"Either it's a wild goose chase or you'll become a Queen to a non-existent people. Who were these Picts anyway?"

"They were the first people, what many think, to inhabit the British Isles, some four thousand years ago. They came over from mainland Europe. Later, they melded with the Celts, mainly in Ireland, Wales and Scotland. Then the Scandinavians, Vikings, came, and that gave another change to our society. It what makes us British, the mix of people. If you add in the French, Dutch and the Saxons, well here we are today."

"Wow, in a nutshell, fantastic, thank you for not boring me."

"That was a simplified version. Something that should suit you," she jibed.

"Ha, Ha, hilarious. So, what do we do when we get there? I mean, at this Ring?"

"Don't have a clue, but I feel confident that someone or something will manifest itself and we'll take it from there."

"Oh, that sounds like a good plan. Stand in the middle of a field and wing it from there. Good, noted. I should be able to handle that."

"Stop it, you idiot. I've had some things happen these last two days, which were significant. More will happen I know, but not exactly how."

They drove in silence for a few miles then Jason said, "You know, your father, before we left, before he left to go to work, he had a word with me."

"I know, I saw you two in the garage. I don't want to know what you talked about and I don't care nor why you mentioned it. That's between you and him. Why bother me. You know it annoys me when they are too over-protective. You trying to be interesting or what?" she said.

Jason threw a glance at her. "I just wanted to say that your father loves you more than anything else in the world. I wish I had parents like that."

"Oh,... thank you," she said sheepishly.

They drove on and made the five pm ferry to Kirkwall, which would arrive at eleven that evening. On the boat Jason called the bed-and-breakfast informing them they had taken the ferry and what time they expected to arrive. It wasn't a problem.

The icy embrace of a late evening in Kirkwall welcomed them. As they drove the few miles to the bed-and-breakfast, Albia thought it funny that they could be driving around any part of the British Isles. The roads, well kept, and the orange street lighting, looked all too familiar. It was night. They could not take in the spectacular and outlandish vista the Orkneys offered. There was no place like it on the planet. They easily found the B&B among the few houses in Stenness and settled down to a good night's sleep, anticipating the morning and discovering the world into which they were hailed.

Chapter 5

The Princess ails

A bright sunny morning welcomed them as they stepped outside, geared up and ready for the trip to the Ring, as they now called it between themselves. They both walked the mile and a half to the site. They took in the stunning scenery, flat, no trees and the few houses dotted around here and there were like intruders upon a stark landscape, pure and beckoning. Albia drank in the aura the place gave out, thinking of her ancestors who lived here four thousand years earlier, living off herds and rudimentary farming, building stone dwellings sunk into the earth to protect them from the harsh winters and the ever blowing wind. Indeed, bushes only existed near buildings, otherwise the wind was too constant to let them get a hold and grow. Even Jason was enjoying the walk, opening his arms out of freedom and lightness. She too felt that and more. As she walked, it was as though the earth spoke to her, whispering lost meanderings to her ear and soul. She felt at home like she had never felt like before. Joy welled up inside her, heart racing away with the sense of nearness, of oneness. Then, as they crossed the Bridge between the two lochs, Stenness and Harray, and paced the earth on the other side, she felt uneasy, a disturbing vibration of animosity. It got worse as they neared the Ring.

"Jason, I'm not feeling too well. It's strange, as though this earth here, this side of the bridge, doesn't want me. Can you feel it?"

"No, I'm fine. Do you want to go back and rest a while by the B&B? You know we're in no hurry."

"No. This has to be done. I don't know what forces are a play, but the farther we go, the more difficult it's getting. It almost hurts to place my feet on the ground," she said as she teetered on the earthen path.

"You mean the nearer we get to that thing?" Jason said, pointing to the Ring up ahead. "Sit down and take a breather. I'll go up ahead and have a look. There's nobody around."

Albia screamed, "No, you're to stay with me, protect me, please."

"Oh yeah, I forgot, I'm your protector. Right. Well, what if I give you a piggyback?" he grinned.

Albia shot him a deathly glance, "Not on your life," she got up and heroically moved forward, one step at a time. Determination showing on her face. Jason wisely let her be, but stayed close by. He remembered the talk her father had given him and the trust entwined in his words. Suddenly Albia fell to one side, Jason's. He caught her just in time to avoid her hitting the ground, her red, golden hair blowing in the chilly breeze.

"I'll carry you, little Princess. We are nearly there."

Albia gave no reply. She was unconscious, to what appeared to Jason. In reality, she was in an induced trance, her soul levitated to a higher existence, elsewhere.

Finally, they made it to the edge of the Ring and Jason was debating with himself if it was a good thing to let her down to the ground. He had no choice, really. She was becoming heavy. With care, he laid her down on the brown, windswept, harsh grass outlining the Ring.

Jason bent down to ensure Albia was ok. She wasn't. Her skin was becoming a lighter shade of grey, her temperature cooler by the minute. Spasms of terror ran through him. She was dying.

But from what? What evil was at work on her? Can he do anything? Panic set in, he trembled. He looked around him. But nobody was here this early on an April morning. Anxiously he shook Albia, hoping she would come around, get her colour back, smile and all would be all right. It was not to be. Rather, under his gentle grasp she was stiff, dying, dead maybe. In hopelessness, he sobbed. For Albia, for her parents and the anguish of not knowing what was happening. Anger welled up inside him against himself. He was useless, as usual. Feeble and clueless, no mighty protector. How could he go back to her parents? How could he look himself in the mirror knowing he let her die? Such a wonderful person. And he did nothing! He stroked her drab hair, his tears lost between the matted strands of her once golden locks. He cried out loud to the earth, to anything, to the universe, for help, to show him a way of saving her. Nothing. Resigned, he laid down beside her, close and placed a gentle arm around her body, sharing her demise, her destitution from such a brief life riddled with unanswered questions. He kissed her hair and shed tears, sharing in her plight. "I will stay with you forever, Albia," he wept.

Chapter 6

The Ring of Brodgar

A while later, Jason was oblivious to how long had passed, an old woman came hobbling up to them with a similarly old cane, making her slow way over the uneven stubbles of grass and bracken.

She cried when she was close enough to distinguish the two on the ground, "What are you two doing?"

Jason stirred and looked up with puffed eyes, "Who are you?"

"Dosen't matter who I am. What are you two doing like that?" she approached and nudged Albia who didn't move.

"Stop that! She's not well," he made a move to protect Albia from the cane.

The old women bent down and saw Albia's features, sick and dying. Then a realisation overwhelmed her, "Sweet heavens, it's her!" she said, quivering. She glanced around, glad no one was in sight. "Quick lad, draw her toward that stone and inside the circle. She needs to touch it. Be careful and be quick."

Puzzled, Jason got up, "What do you mean, she needs the stone?"

"She is losing her life spirit, her ethereal is leaving her. You need to stop that and the only way is to get her into that ring! Do it!" she said with surprising force.

Bewildered and sad, Jason looked at Albia, her lifeless body sinking into the ground. He raised his arms in hopelessness. "She's dying. That won't save her."

The old women made her painful way toward Jason and looked up to him, bright blue eyes staring into his soul. Jason could have sworn he saw galaxies rotate within her irises. She said nothing. She didn't need to.

Shocked, Jason said, "Right, get her into the Ring, right." He gently picked her stiff body up and stepped the two feet into the ring. Immediately Albia gave a deep guttural splutter, like someone coming up for air, as spasms shuddered through her body. Gasping she said, "Where am I?"

Jason let out a sigh of relief at her revival. The old women came up to them and said, "You are where you need to be dear," she drew closer and looked her in the eyes, "Oh my, you are so beautiful. Lay her down, son," she ordered Jason, who complied.

"What's happening? She was dying and now she's coming around. I only just stepped a few feet into this ring," he said with a grunt as he laid her down on the ground again.

The old woman ignored him and intoned, "Of all the lives, generations and millennia, and this happens in my lifetime," she then raised her eyes skyward, "Thank you, thank you, oh blessed spirits of the ether," she said with unabashed joy. Lowering her gaze back to Albia, who was now seated against a stone pillar, she added, "Son, give her something to drink and some food if you have any. If not, I'll fetch something."

Jason knelt down and opened his bag and drew out a thermos and a piece of cheese, "Here, take this, you'll feel better after," he said after having poured a hot coffee into a small cup.

Albia looked at them, "What happened? I felt elsewhere, absent, I don't know how long. And who are you?" she added, looking cautiously at the woman leaning against her cane.

"My name is Eldred, I am the last of a long, and I mean a long line of Watchers."

"Watchers?" asked Jason.

"For millennia, my ancestors have lived here in nearby houses to watch over the Ring," she gave a reverent glance around her, "We knew somebody would come to claim the heir of the Picts."

Albia, fidgeting, said, "And what has that got to do with me? I am just a nobody from York. A little girl, some would say. I wouldn't, but what happened here? When I passed out?"

"My dear, there are wicked spirits lying in wait here to hinder the one. They recognized you immediately, even if you think you are quite normal. You are not."

"What happened then? You mentioned her ethereal was leaving her?" said Jason.

Eldred turned toward Albia again, "What is you name, dear?"

"Albia."

"Of course, it would be. My late husband told me about you and his visit to your parents. So they adopted your proper name. This is wonderful."

"You mean that man who came to my parents when I was born? He is your late husband?"

"Yes, dear. He passed away five years ago," she looked into the distance. "Alfred was a good man. He roamed these parts, hoping to find you. Sometimes he went well into England. That's when he found you. He was so excited. May I ask you a question?"

"Yes, of course," Albia said, getting up, feeling much stronger.

"How did you know to come here?"

Albia rummaged in her coat pocket and drew out the acorn, "Here, this fell on me a few days ago."

Eldred took it delicately and scrutinized the acorn, holding it within inches of her failing eyes, "Ah indeed, your calling. Wonderful, dear."

Jason interrupted their discussion, "So why did she get better once we were in the Ring? I mean, it was like magic."

"It would seem so to you, my boy, but here she is protected from those spirits. They cannot penetrate the circle. Those stones you see are defences against them. In the beginning, there were sixty stones around the Pledge. Now, sadly, only twenty-seven remain. Their protection has weakened over the centuries. But enough to protect you still," she finished admiring Albia, "You are so beautiful."

"Thank you, Eldred. I don't feel it. This is all… otherworldly. The Pledge?"

"Otherworldly is the right word. There is a hidden world of spirits. Few can see them, yet they are there and have their influence. But now you are safe. The Pledge is a golden necklace which belonged, or should I say belongs to Albia the Pict Princess, or rather her spirit, which dwells with you. It was brought over by the first settlers of these islands over four thousand years ago. It comes from the region and peoples called Yamnaya, some of whom migrated to our parts. Their origin is roughly between the Caspian and

Black Sea. The Pledge is a symbol of the Earth and the Spirit. It is what ties us to the Earth," she finished with bright yet stern eyes.

"Great, but we can't stay here all our lives," gasped Jason, "How do we get out without Albia falling ill again? I don't want her to go through that again."

"The Pledge, necklace, will protect you so long as Albia wears it, or at least touches it. It's concealed about a sheep's depth under a buried stone in the centre of this Ring. You need to get it."

"What? Dig it out?" murmured Jason.

"Yes, but not now during the day. There will be people roaming around soon, and seeing a couple of tourists digging a hole in the middle of an ancient ruin will not go down well. You'll need to come back tonight, late, when everyone is inside. Bring what you need and a torch."

Albia licked her lips in uncertainty, "And what about getting back to our room? I'll be drawn down by those spirits again."

"Yeah, we're not going through that again. I won't let that happen," Jason said bravely.

"You could carry her to the bridge. That should do. Once over the other side, you'll be far enough away not to be attacked," Eldred said.

"Attacked!" startled Jason.

"Those spirits can be quite nasty. Remember, for millennia they have waited just for this moment. They want the Pledge. They think it'll liberate them. Which it won't. Those forces can use nature as well, to thwart you."

"As well?" Jason said, raising his eyebrow.

"Well, of course. Albia can also use nature to protect her. She just needs to learn how to do it. Listen Albia, you have that power, you must have witnessed some happenings around you to testify to that. Use it now, touch the grass below you and wish with all your sweet heart something to happen. Try."

"Eh, I don't know what to wish for," she said, looking forlornly at the grass.

"Kneel dear and touch the grass."

Albia, after a moment's pause, knelt. She then placed her small hands on the rough grass.

Nothing happened. She looked up to Eldred and shrugged her shoulders.

Eldred shook her head, "No dear, you are going about it the wrong way. Show love to the earth, the grass under your feet, feel its energy and reply to its yearning."

Jason looked on with unhidden derision, "Nothing will happen, I can tell you."

Albia leant forward and placed her hands onto the ground. Then she laid her face, flirting with the grass blades, and whispered, "I love you. You are me and I you." Immediately the grass grew higher and greener, leaning into her face from all sides, caressing her features, protecting and loving. Albia, startled, rose and looked at Eldred with open eyes.

"Darling, you are the only person who can receive such love from Mother Earth. Those other spirits out there only wield their power over it. They are not in communion. They attempt to master it. With your love, the Earth will respond in kind. You don't need to give orders. She will know what to do. Have faith, have confidence, and you shall prevail."

"Wow, that was pretty snazzy," said Jason while packing the thermos into his bag. "Do you feel up to it, Albia? Or do you want me to carry you?" he sniggered.

Albia shot him a warning stare, "I'll be alright. Let's go. Eldred, thank you for everything. You have explained a lot. We shall come back tonight. Will you be here?"

"Thank you, dear, but no, I won't be here for you. I do not go out at night. The Spirits have too much power over me if I venture out. They know I am a Watcher. I am vulnerable, more so with Alfred gone. Sorry. But I live in that house over there," she said, pointing to a small stone building a few furlongs away, "If need be, you can come to me. Now get going and may the Earth protect you."

"Thank you, Eldred," Albia said as she kissed her forehead.

Jason waved and stepped outside the ring.

Chapter 7

The Spirits of hate and jealousy

Albia followed Jason with a first tentative step. She looked all around her, nothing, then sighted Eldred giving an encouraging gesture to go. She moved forward with courage and determination, Jason was already a few feet ahead. When she was only a cow's length from one stone and outside, the earth suddenly trembled, shook and roared in anger.

Jason looked back with a forlorn look of surprise and loss. He was being engulfed into a large crevasse which had opened up under his feet. Albia, looking on with terror, ran toward him but, suddenly, a mound of dark earth rose in front of her, blocking her view of him. Panic rang through her body, making her shiver in fear. What can she do? She fretted to herself as her vision, blurred by the trembling ground under her feet, made her scream in terror. A second later, she got hold of herself and shouted, "Jason, hold on, hold on. I am coming."

Something, something within, called to her, taking over her body. She laid down and sung to the soil now bubbling up with fury all around her. She sang from her soul. An unknown song, in a strange language, enchanting and melodic. It immediately calmed the sea of broiling earth, rent asunder the mound, and opened a path to Jason. The Earth responded to her love.

She gasped at the sight, Jason was half buried and sinking fast! She crawled on all fours to get to him and gave her hand, stretching down over the liquid earth. "Jason, take my hand!" she cried.

Jason looked up, sad and resigned. He was being taken, buried alive, eyes disappearing under the soil. Albia's reach, already at full stretch, was getting further away from Jason's blind groping hand. Horrified, Albia looked on helplessly, screaming, crying and bleeding her soul for the man who had accompanied her on this foolish journey. She too slid down, slowly being engulfed by the moving earth.

She heard a cry from behind, Eldred, what was she saying? It was unintelligible, drowned in the din of the seething earth. Then she caught a word, a single word, KISS. Yes! That was it, Kiss. But Kiss?

Kiss what? Then her inner self welled up again and possessed her body. Still reaching down to Jason, now disappeared under the earth with only his hand flaying wildly above him, she bowed her head, her golden hair flowing over the ground like the sun warming a lost, cold sparrow, and kissed the earth. A kiss of love and oneness with nature herself, soul kissing its very essence.

Suddenly, she heard a crack beneath her. A branch grew around Jason, growing bigger and thicker, then several branches slid out, enveloping him until it raised him up to the sky. Then they bent to lay him down on the ground next to Albia. Jason was gasping for air, wrapped in a cobweb of twigs and branches which opened up and freed him from its firm hold. He coughed and spluttered dirt as he scrambled out of Nature's nest. Albia was likewise cradled in a web of small branches which had grown under her like a bed, lifting her away from the sliding pit of earth. She crawled forward and wrapped her arms around Jason. "Oh Jason, Jason. You're alive! Come, we must go back to the Ring. It will protect us." They both scrambled back to a horrified Eldred.

"Quickly dears, get inside!" she said with her weak voice, "Before they do something else."

Once inside, the ground outside quietened down, although the terrain looked as though it had had a giant plough go through it. Nothing was recognisable, mounds, crevasses and craters dotted the area all around the stones. Within, all was calm, untouched. The stones proudly stood in staunch defiance of the hate and jealousy dwelling in the depths of the surrounding earth.

Jason, sitting against a stone next to Albia, drew out a bottle of water from his sack and handed it to Albia, "I don't know what to say. That was terrifying. I don't know what you did, but you were fantastic Albia. Thank you. I thought I was a gonna there."

"I don't know either," she said looking up to Eldred who was standing over them with a triumphant smile, "You did it Albia, with your love, you did it. See what I mean, once you learn how to use your gift, wisely, you will become a true Princess. You need to feel your heart, your love, and your earth will protect you as it sees fit. I am so proud of you Albia, Princess Albia."

"I feel little to be proud of at the moment. We nearly died there. What are the spirits you talk about? Who are they?" she said, taking a long gulp of water and handing the bottle to Jason.

"They were invaders long after the Picts had settled here. The Picts had a soft, peaceful way of life, living off the land, the animals and crafting wonderful art. When those barbarians came and destroyed their peace, there was no going back. These stones were primarily erected to be in harmony with their gods. If you notice the sun, at certain times of the year, it is aligned with the stones. There are several such sites dotted around the northern British Isles and a few in the south. They all honour Mother earth, the universe and the ethereal benevolent spirits that gender the love given by our earth. The sea with its gift of food and travel. The earth, food, shelter and beauty. The animals, a source of inspiration to men. The sky, sun and moon all contributing to a wonderful place to live and enjoy. Unfortunately, man being what he is, has diverted and adulterated it. Using its power to dominate, control and benefit not only from Nature but also his fellow man. The King of the Picts, Albia's father, was a kind man, reigning with wisdom and love.

When the invaders came it was all destroyed and finally, after many centuries, the Picts melded with other nations such as the Celts, who were also like them, sensitive and in phase with nature, at one with the earth. But in the meantime, the damage was done. The invaders were in search of the Pledge, of course. They knew it would give them the power of everything, existence, and they sought it with brutality. But the Princess Albia, through her infinite kindness and wisdom, hid it within this circle and cast a spell, or a wish to nature if you like, to the stones to protect it. There are similar items in other rings elsewhere."

"And you, the watchers? How did you come about, I mean your lineage?" said Jason, shaking off the dirt from his clothes.

"The Princess ordained a family to watch over the Pledge and help if the blessed one should arise in a future time. It's a secret well kept for centuries and centuries. I feel so honoured that today, after millennia, I can help. I have no descendants, so with me, the watchers, for this ring, die out. You came just in time!" she smiled, "Thank you, Princess."

"Don't call me a Princess, I don't feel like one," she said with a loving smile to Eldred, "Thank you for guidance. Without that, I don't know what would have happened."

"Speaking of which, what happens now?" Jason said, "We're stuck. I'm not going through that again," he shuddered as he thought of the earth sucking him in.

Chapter 8

The dig, the policemen and the car

Eldred looked around them, concerned, "This event will draw attention. It won't be long before someone sees this mess and will alert the authorities- "

"What the bloody ´ell have you done now, Witch?" shouted an elderly man walking through the tumbled mess of the land around the Ring, interrupting her.

"Keep away Donald and mind your own business and I am not a Witch!" Eldred said, looking guardedly at the approaching man.

"My eye, you're not. Look at this. What happened?"

"Nothing to bother your simple mind, now go away."

"Listen, Witch, this concerns us all. I have already phoned through to Jack in Kirkwall, so they'll be here in a few ticks. Police, the Council, and they'll want answers. You are so in deep trouble, at last.

Well-deserved, if you ask me. You meddle too much with your cants and rituals."

"You are ignorant, Donald, and stupid," she turned her back to him and addressed Jason, "You'll have to be quick, the Police will be here soon and take you all away. You need to get the Pledge for Albia. Can you do that? Now?" she stared into his eyes, galaxies rotating in hypnotising fluidity.

"Eh, I can try. Let me get something from my bag, I've brought one of those military fold-up shovels. Where is the centre then?"

Eldred, ignoring shouts from Donald, made her slow, painful way to the centre of the Ring. "There, under that stone half protruding from the ground. It's my job to make sure it's always kept free from the earth, or part of it. It's quite a big stone, so you'll have to dig around a bit."

"Ok, let me get started," Jason said as he drove the spade through the thick grass around the stone, "So a sheep's depth, eh? Right."

Albia moved up fretting, "I can see some cars coming over the bridge Jason, make it quick, there'll be here in a few minutes."

"I'm doing my best. This earth is thick with grass."

"Ha ha, here they come. You're in for it now, Witch," Donald gloated as he looked on, "Desecrating an ancient site. Finally, we'll be able to get rid of you and your games."

"Shut up, idiot," said Eldred with surprising vehemence.

Five cars drew up on the road close to the Ring, two of which were police cars. Several people got out shouting, looking at the disaster circling the ring. It took them all a moment to realise what had happened, although they had no real idea.

They came ambling around the mounds and cracks in the earth, annoyed and gesticulating with their arms to Jason who was fiendishly digging away.

"Stop that right now! And I want ID," shouted one police officer.

Eldred hobbled over to meet them before they came to the Ring's edge, "Stop right there, we are unearthing some property which belongs to this young girl. This is beyond you all."

Two of the police officers brushed past her, making a B line for Jason. Albia looked on, frightened. Jason would not make it before the men got him. The other people came into the Ring to confront Eldred and Albia. It was a mistake.

"I am the mayor of this Island and I demand you to stop right now!" A man said with authority.

"Not going to happen Sir," said Albia, "There is a necklace down there which belongs to me, I am an heir of the Princess Albia of the Picts," she said proudly.

"That Witch led them into it, it's all her fault, with her castings and spells. I am glad you came in time to stop them-" Suddenly the earth within the Ring vibrated. Everyone stopped their progress and looked around, bewildered. "Told ye so for years. This Witch has been stirring up trouble for years." He had just finished his sentence when a growth of grass wrapped around his legs and then his body, holding him still. The two policemen, reaching for Jason, were sinking into the earth while the surrounding grass grew over their heads, holding them painlessly in the earth. Jason looked with snarky bemusement and continued to dig with all his force, slowly being able to dislodge the stone with his shovel.

"What's happening here?" said someone not yet held in grass and twigs.

"You are meddling in things you don't understand. It's as simple as that. Now calm down and wait patiently. Albia is retrieving her right to an object destined to her for millennia."

"Fucking Witch," mumbled Donald through the thick bracken and grass. Eldred sniggered with unhidden pleasure.

"I got the stone away now!" shouted Jason, "But I still need to dig a bit more earth. A sheep's depth, you say. Right." He finished as he got back to work on the soil.

"You will pay for this, Mrs MacPherson," said an employee of the local council. "You know that anything found on Scottish soil is the property of the State."

"Only if it doesn't belong to someone else. Which is the case here." She beamed, looking over at Jason who was making excellent progress. Then suddenly a car drove over the uneven ground, making its way toward the Ring, aiming between two stones. Someone was trying to stop Jason with their car.

"Jason!" cried Albia, "Look out, that car is heading for you!"

Jason looked up as the car, now within the circle, picked up its bumpy speed, and drove straight for him. He stood stock still, panic-stricken and wrought with fear. Not a few feet away from him, a tree suddenly sped upwards out of the ground with such a speed that the driver had no time to change course. It collided with it, halting its progress immediately. Then a wrath of branches and twigs grew up over the car, covering it in a dense thicket. The occupant could not open the doors. Trapped, the woman screamed. Nobody could go to her aid. All the newcomers were wrapped up in a thicket or had their legs steadfastly held with heavy wooden branches. The sight was strange. Albia smiled inwardly and moved to Jason.

"How's it going?"

"Nearly there,... there!" he exclaimed as his shovel hit a buried stone, "That must be it!" he quickly dug around the deeper stone and eased it up so he could grab it. "Got it!" he grunted. It revealed a square flat stone, not one foot on each side. "That must be it Albia, this is your show, you need to unearth it. It's been there for thousands of years."

She waited until Jason crawled out of the shallow hole to let Albia get in. Eldred had made her way toward them with expectant eyes, anticipating the wonder about to be released.

Chapter 9

The Pledge

Albia bent to get a good grip on the flat stone, but it was heavy. "Jason, can you help, please? It's quite heavy."

Jason stepped down and took hold of one side and they both lifted, then placed the flagstone on the side. Albia looked down to a small square made of stone. Within was a mass of disintegrating cloth. She placed her hand on the substance which gave way and turned into dust. She then entered her fingers in the pile and touched a hard object.

"I think I have found it," she said, looking up at Eldred with a smile.

"How long did you say Eldred? Four thousand years? Amazing," said Jason as he knelt to get a closer look. "Go on Albia, it's yours, take it out."

She took hold of the object and pulled it out of the stone box and held it up to the bright afternoon light. "It's heavy," is all that she said.

"I can't see anything with all that gunk around it," Jason said. Eldred was looking on eagerly.

Albia shook it gently. The cloth fell away to reveal a bright golden pendant with a heavy golden chain. The pendant was simple, round with small black stones set into the rim. In the middle was an engraving, deeply cut, of a double beast surrounding a stylish design. Someone magnificently executed it with the finest details clearly cut, the gold lighting up the pendant.

"It's marvellous," exclaimed Albia who had not yet touched it, still holding it over the mass of cloth still stuck to it.

"Oh my dear, this is wonderful. I am so proud of you. Of all, you are deserving. I know you will use this wisely," said Eldred, holding her hands together in glee.

"It's quite pretty, I'll admit, but clunky no?" Jason suggested.

"No, it's perfect." Albia said with lit up golden eyes.

"Give that object to me!" said the Mayor, still held in a thicket, "Or else I will destroy you!"

Albia stopped looking at the pendant and turned to the man and strode up to him. "You are misguided and led by your own selfish desires and fears. This is beyond anything your present state can conceive." She turned to Jason and Eldred and touched the gold... immediately the air bristled around her. An aura of white, blue light shone from her body, making her semi-transparent. To Jason, it seemed she had grown in stature. Eldred saw the love she had in her become visible. She was beautiful, the essence of the earth, the meaning of love. Meaning for her existence and her future.

When Albia looked at Jason and Eldred, her eyes shone, now blue bright, like diamonds, piercing yet meek. Possessed with the energy of earth, the energy of the Ether, she felt those thousands upon thousands of sleeping Ethers, waking and crying in joy to share such a moment of accomplishment. She felt the Ethers outside the Ring shrink back into the depths. She felt an essence swirling within. Nature was talking to her, communicating. It said, "Princess Albia of the Picts, you are the vector of our love for humanity. Go, show and bless this world with our gift. Show them the love from which the earth was made. The power of love is infinite. Release theirs, which has been locked down by the wicked for centuries. The Ethers will accompany you wherever you go. Show no fear, be bold and coerce the world back to reason and love. You are not alone. We love you, as we know you do us."

Everyone heard this statement, gob smacked in awe. The Thickets and twigs and grass all receded back into the earth while the mounds around the Ring drew flat and calm. It released the car, freeing the woman who indicted, "What the fucking hell was that? I'll have you. Officers, arrest that woman, now! She'll pass the rest of her life in prison. I'll make sure," she said, spitting on the ground. Ill advised. A blade of grass grew up to her eye level and caressed her cheek before receding. "Aargh, what was that? Get them now!"

Nobody was inclined to move except Donald, who sidled over to Eldred. He looked into her eyes. "I am so, so sorry Eldred," he cried, sobbed and sang his heart out in grief.

"Don't be silly Donald, you were always playing the mean guy, but deep inside you, lays a teddy bear. I know, I have always known," she smiled and kissed him.

Jason moved up to Albia, who was still holding the Pendant, and said with a smile, "Put it on."

She did, with purpose, with feeling, with all her soul: she laid the chain around her gentle white neck, placed the pendant against her chest and took in a deep breath, refining, cleansing, purifying. With glee and celebration, she twirled around and around waving her arms out and high, embracing life, embracing love, embracing all...

The Fox

Mike Lees

I first became aware that I had accepted, even from my youth, many false opinions for true, and that consequently what I afterwards based on such principles was highly doubtful: and from that time I was convinced of the necessity of undertaking once in my life to rid myself of all the opinions I had adopted, and of commencing anew the work of building from the foundation,...

Rene Descartes, French Philosopher

The rational mind is a humble servant. The intuitive mind, the faithful gift. We have created a society that honours the servant and forgotten the gift.

Albert Einstein

Chapter 1

Cogito Ergo Sum (I think, hence I am)

John felt alien. Mayhem was all around him as he sat on the sofa watching his two children, TV blasting out nonsense and his wife on the phone to one of her friends, talking loudly, compound nonsense. Lost. No past and no future and the present? Well, he looked around him again, no help there. Why exist? Why beget children, why fall in love? What advancement is there in occupying himself with such fruitless, never-ending pursuits? Why? Why? Why go to work, earn money to let it fall into that bottomless pit called life? A life without end, without an aim except to perennate the species. A knot curled up in his stomach, bile rising, a mental quiver weighing down his existence. He entered the kitchen, to make a coffee, something to do, to bide his time, to distract him. It was not helping though. Whilst waiting for the water to boil, he stared at the boiler slowly changing the molecules in the water to boiling point; his mobile rang, drawing him from his reverie. He drew it out of his back pocket, Dan, ok.

"Dan? Hi,"

"Hey John, Gary and I are going down Snob's, wanna come?"

A welcome distraction. "Yeah, what time?"

"Now, I'm meeting him there straight away."

"Ok, see you later, bye."

John closed his phone and interrupted the boiler, glad to wield his power of decision over it. *I can stop the boiling water or not, I decide, I have that power.* It made him chuckle internally. Pathetic, reduced to mundane, inconsequential decisions. His family, his job and the house, set a grid to obey, follow like an automaton. Go through the actions, try not to think, not to question, just do.

Obey his wife and children, obey his company, his boss, obey the government, obey the tax forms, obey the road signals, obey Christmas and birthdays, obey the bills, obey showering every day, obey brushing his teeth, obey sleep. Ah, sleep… one of the few things he loved. To curl up and sleep, let his body and mind drift off to wherever they wanted to go, obeying nothing, listening to nothing, being aware of nothing… bliss. He heard shouting from the living room, David and Jane were quibbling over the remote again. He could sense the hate emanating from the room. Hate over a remote, over nonsense, emotion over… everything, over meaning. He needed meaning, meaning to live, to die, to exist, to not exist. What is meaning? Elusive yet so necessary to exist. Who was he? Why did he exist?... He watched the water simmering down, returning to still water again from the frenzy of bubbles and steam. He needed to do that as well, but how? How could he simmer down, be at peace with himself, accept, be docile? Did he want to? Again, why? Yet, who was he to question life? He should be happy, a family, job, friends… yet… yet… turmoil, angst and floundering, a fish caught at low tide in a puddle too small for it. The sun blearing down, drying its scales, whitening its eyes and sticking its fins to its body. He felt like that fish, caught unawares. De-wombed to a nightmare, a trap! He unconsciously looked from right to left in the kitchen. No escape. The pub, ok, that'll have to do, for now…

* * *

The third beer, the table sticky with spilt amber, the smell of ale, the sound of laughter, meaningless talk. Talk about things, not the why of things. An empty, passage of time, waiting for death.

Home, quite, dark, late… He crept into bed, burping. Curled up and thought…

Where is the road, the road to open skies and weightlessness? A maze which others called a labyrinth. A lie, no way out, no sensible path, just dead ends, failures, emptiness. Who was he to his wife, his children; security. Was he secure? Could he batten down those dark shadows encroaching on his joy? Joy. Well, that was a funny word. Born of ignorance and stupidity. But how can a man, aware of his predicament, be happy, joyous? To think is to exist, someone said, a French philosopher? But for him, it was a malediction, a plague, poisoning existence. Numbing awareness drawing over him as the years pass. He cried. He slept, but little.

Individually there has developed a widespread feeling of helplessness and despair faced with what seems to be an overwhelming mass of disparate social forces, going beyond the control and even the comprehension of the human beings who are caught up in it.

David Bohm, Wholeness and the Implicate Order, 1980

Chapter 2

Children's playground

A shoe scuffed against his cubicle. Without looking up, he knew it was Gary, his way of asserting himself.

"Hi John, the Boss wants to see you as soon as you get in, he said it's urgent," he said smiling.

"I've been here half an hour already, why didn't you tell me then?"

"Ah, you know, busy and all," he strode off toward his own cubicle.

Obey, obey, obey. He got up and made his slow way up the stairs to the third floor. He met Mr Johnson in the corridor.

"Ah good, John, please follow me into my office," he said with a grim stare, "Close the door and take a seat."

"Gary said it was urgent, he only told me a few minutes ago. What can I do?"

"Delicate John, delicate. Apparently Mrs Wainwright, on the fourth, accounts, had a word with her team leader, who came to me, naturally. It would appear that you threatened her in the lift yesterday. It quite upset her."

"I don't know what you mean, I said hello to her. That's all."

"She felt aggressed John. This is serious. You know we're coming up for an audit next week. Those revisers will be all over the place. We can't afford to have a scandal in our books. The shareholders, John. Do I have to spell it out? Mrs Wainwright doesn't want to take this any further, nor do I. You've been with us, what? Five years. You are a valuable asset for our company, but this. I don't know how to handle it the best way."

So it has come to that, eh? Walking the tightrope of social values, forever thinner, forever higher.

Imaginary scares in a world of fantasy. A children's playground.

"I did nothing, I just said hello. What else can I say?"

"Best not say anymore. I'll have a talk with her team leader, try to calm things down. Avoid causing trouble again, otherwise there will be consequences. Do you understand me, John?"

"I do, but I cannot see what I did wrong."

"Therein lays the problem John, if you don't see it, the situation may be worse than we think. Our image has to be clean. Those revisers and our shareholders, remember? I can't afford that, for sure, and I don't want to pay for something somebody else did. So keep it tight and be careful. You may go."

The grey cloth covered cubicle closed in on him, a vice, unrelenting. How did he get into this state?

Was it the car accident last year? Bringing actual values to bear. Making him think. A novelty, for sure. That accident had lifted some scales from his eyes. He saw things in a different light, harsher, clearer, questioned things. His life, his existence, his emotions, his balance and hold on life. What did it all mean? And now accused of aggressing a woman in a lift. What values has the world adopted? What railway track are they on? Certainly not the same train as he. He felt defragmented, no fil rouge in his life to guide him during the storm. No lighthouse. Nothing. Him and the world. He felt suddenly tired. Weak.

"Hey,"

Gary. "Yes," he said numbly.

"What did he want with you?"

"A talk."

"Don't believe you. Anyway, can you take this up to the fourth? They're waiting for them to close this month's accounts. Thanks," he said, dumping a pile of spreadsheets onto his desk as he left. He turned back, "Lunch later?"

John nodded automatically.

He picked up the pile and went to the lift. Getting out on the fourth, he passed a set of cubicles with four women chatting. They frowned at him as he passed.

* * *

"Take a seat, John. What did I say, no more games? Why did you go up there? To intimidate her? She was distraught. Her leader is calming her down as we speak. He's trying his best to avoid any unpleasantness," said Johnson as his phone rang, "Yes,... he's here with me now. What?... I see. Good idea and a suitable compromise. I'll inform John right away. Tell Mrs Wainwright she need not fret anymore. Thanks." He slammed his phone down and gave a stern look at John. "Mrs Wainwright will let things be if you are at least suspended. Otherwise she will create a stink. We can't allow that. Therefore, we are suspending you henceforth pending such decisions that we may take. I am sorry John, but you went too far despite my warnings. I'll keep you informed, but for now, please leave the building."

Chapter 3

The Road

Home. Empty, tinny, soulless. He went upstairs and sat on the bed. Needing to think, yet the muddling fog in his mind kept cloaking any genuine attempt to see clearly a situation which had got completely out of hand. Shivers kidnapped his body like a marionette, unable to halt, nor wanting to, the fever taking over him. He wanted to suffer, to hurt. How? He laid down in a foetus position on the bed, shutting the world out behind pale skin. Seeking succour in his thoughts. To no avail. He needed to suffer like an athlete training for the Olympics. No other choice but to go through the pain if you want to achieve anything meaningful.

Meaningful = Pain = Meaningful. Suffering. An idea came to him, the cabin. Scotland.

* * *

He left home the next morning with his bags, leaving behind his screaming wife and bewildered kids. Nobody understood. Nor should they. He had lost all control of himself and his life. He was on a last bet to save everything. The alternative would be oblivion. He walked down the drive to the car with detached determination, certain he was following the only road open to him, to salvation. Salvation, a good word, but what does it mean? To save or be saved. And from what? Who was going to save him? It was clear: Nobody... except himself. This gave him resolve to continue despite leaving behind a family wrought with panic and frustration. They couldn't understand. Wouldn't. Shouldn't. This was his El Alamein, he would not let the tides of despair overwhelm him, and the cabin will be his battleground!

* * *

The road, January, sleet, grey, dirt, trucks, idiots. He drove into a large Morrison's for provisions. At peace in his car, entering the parking sucked him into a vortex of society: bland, obedient, functioning. He parked his car between the lines, put money in a slot to get his caddy, like so many others. A family, two kids and a baby, had arrived at the same time as he. He followed them into the store. Music, bargain announces, lights, colours, numbers. Everything was a numbers game: Get 3 for 2, half price, 20% off, multi-packs, special offers. They all called out to him, vying for his attention, occupying his thoughts, taking over. He saw the family, debating the 3 for 2's, caught in the snare. A snare by necessity, money pressure, it all came down to that. We are led by money, surrendering our existence to an imaginary construct: Money. Unreal, a concept, an idea, a collective belief. The Emperor's New Clothes: A belief in the invisible, a belief in what others tell you. People alienated upon an island in the middle of islands, isolated to fend for themselves. What happened to community, sharing, exchange, bartering, giving? Words that no longer describe our society. A society prone to self. No one will help, help yourself, be better, be best, ruthless, unkind, selfish. New Age chain-mail to resist the barbarous hordes of empathy and love. Or so the social subliminal and never spoken dictate says. Another word which has gone onto the slag heap.

Empathy. Who wants empathy? What use in our society? What can one do with a now blunt tool called empathy?

He looked at the family and felt empathy for them. Warriors on the battlefield, fighting, losing, dying. Forgotten. A lone island, screaming across a cold sea, never being heard, never seen, never saved, no salvation. So where comes this word: happiness? How can lost warriors find happiness? The family moved on, counting the dimes. Magicians, all of them, yet unaware. Doing the impossible in the face of oppressive mockery. Mockery. The rich, do they care, in their safe houses? Politicians, do they care, in their Ivory towers of disdain? The Taxman will throw you into prison if you do not give over your money. Highwaymen, ready to take your life for your money, impervious to the annihilation, serving only the construct. No room for empathy, only lust, thievery and power.

The construct. The construct. The construct. The new mantra.

Our task must be to free ourselves from the prison by widening our circle of compassion to embrace all living creatures and the whole of nature in its beauty... The true value of a human being is determined primarily by the measure and the sense in which they have obtained liberation from the self.

Albert Einstein

Chapter 4

The Cabin

It was late as he drove through the stark yet wonderful countryside in the western part of Scotland, making his way to Loch Schiel. The cabin, leftover from his Grandfather, snuggled on the southern banks of the Loch, had a beautiful view of the Loch and the mountains opposite on the northern side. The summit of Rois-Bheinn looking over him from the distance. The modest forest behind the cabin felt good and motherly, hugging the loch, drawing life from its icy, dark waters.

John pushed a sigh of relief when he silenced the car a few feet from the cabin. Silence, deafening silence, tingling in his ears. Bliss, nothingness. He, the cabin, nature. He sat for twenty minutes drinking the view, appreciating his environment, waking up. For an instant, he caught himself not thinking. An alien concept these last few months. He knew he had done the right thing in coming here. A far cry from the office, the TV, shops, obligations. Was he running away? No, he thought, he was going head on towards his nemesis, his self, a confrontation few dare.

* * *

He drew in the late afternoon air, deep, cleansing, then expelled, purging his tensions. It was getting dark, cold. He walked leisurely around the cabin, inspecting. Fair order, but the stack of wood on one side had fallen down. A few tools leant up against the wood strewn on the floor. He marvelled at the soft, spongy earth beneath his feet. Seasons of pine needles. A welcome kindness in this harsh land. A reminder of earth and its benevolence, its love. He smiled.

The road, concealed from the cabin, lay some two hundred yards behind, hidden in the forest. Few people ventured along the road, and less so in January. He was alone. Alone, yet his inner universe was busy, bubbling over with excitement and apprehension. It was down to him. His job. His challenge, that many at his office, would not even entertain. Alone, for them, meant sad, lonely, unsociable, unfriendly. An enemy to their mirage of values forced upon them by society and those who wield power. Damn them. This is my fight. My being naked before me. This thought reminded him of what Mr Johnson had said: there will be consequences. He laughed. Our entire society is based on fear. Not love, nor kindness, nor justice. Magnanimous, an ancient word, once useful, now forgotten, unused, banished. Like so many useful yesteryear terms. Our society has grown out of them. Other words have taken their place: Equality, Tolerance, Unity. Such words, supposedly positive, had become like your money for the taxman, waylaid and turned to favour more spurious objectives by those hidden in the shadows. Equality: a lie to subdue the masses, vomited by the rich and powerful, by those who are not equal. A lie to hide behind, render guilty any who object. Similar to Tolerance: Accept the absurd lest you be cancelled. Accept injustice in the name of justice. Accept hypocrisy. Unity: Be as we say, be one under our banner. Unity: being the antonym to diversity and freedom of culture and mind. The right to be different. What did Shakespeare say: "Tis' a pageant to keep us in false gaze." Fuck the pageants of lies and devious greed. Black is black. Black is not white. Yet we live in a society of double-talk: the media, adverts, political speeches and so-called victim groups. We are drowning in them, sinking to unfathomable depths to join the carcasses of those who dared object, strewn along the seabed. Slain witnesses to a society in full denial.

* * *

First things first. Get the stove going, heat, light, oil lamps here, no electricity. Get the provisions in, then prepare something hot. Shake the bed linen. That will do for tonight. Bed with a book, pulp fiction and fact, a wonderland of the mind. A book, what a marvel, yet powers stir in the murky depths, to cloak the light. Clouds forming, the Unity, closing in to deprive people of wonderment and error. He read The Hobbit, a vista of human traits beautifully portrayed through the eyes of a humble. Sleep came when it came, peaceful and quiet, deep and free.

"Goodbye," said the fox. "And now here is my secret, a very simple secret: It is only with the heart that one can see rightly; what is essential is invisible to the eye."

Antoine de Saint-Exupéry

Chapter 5

The Fox

He lay there in the sumptuous embrace of half sleep. The cold encroaching through the linen, light waning through the window, a talisman of hope and invincibility. He smiled and thought of the many chores he'd set himself to do for this first day. Refreshing simple immediate thoughts, cleansing his mind. He lay his bare feet on the cold lino floor… Stir the embers, shake the world, and chase the spiders. The world, his world, his universe, his existence was coming to life.

The old cast-iron stove gave a warming glow through the opened shutters, life-sustaining warmth. Something real and honest... and simple. So unassuming, a fire, a fire to glow in the soul, the genesis of birth, healing the injuries of remembrances, melting the ice of judgement. It felt so, so good: a fire, a blanket over his shoulders and a cup of coffee clasped between his chilled hands.

He heated a pot of water and poured it into the kitchen sink, took a flannel and begun a purifying wash. Each wipe of the flannel flaking away the tension, easing the nerves and calming those fiends within. He drained his angst down the sink and hung his purifier on a cord drooped behind the stove. Several spiders were pondering his motions during this time, sharing the act, taking part in the renewal of his self. They skittered here and there as he began to dress. He then attempted a good sweep of the floor with an old, too old, broom that his Grandfather had certainly used. One of many items here stooped in history, in memorial. Each gesture brought him back to his youth, a kid sharing this very cabin with that great man. Another unsuspected benefit and agent to cleanse the wells of fear and hopelessness.

All the while, during these chores, he never thought of the world outside. Engrossed in these simple acts captured his senses, reviving the he. Who he was in reality compared to what the world made him be. An adventurer, hacking through a sweltering jungle of deception and non-truths. A hunter, seeking the animal of salvation, seeking himself. A true and fearless broom-wielding predator, eliminating the superfluous of life. Uncovering the essence, the why, the nexus of existence. He looked ruefully at the on-looking spiders and wondered... he would let them be, companions on the road, witnesses.

The cold sun glistened on the lake, berthing a myriad of stars, each one speaking, each one telling a tale. Rois-Bheinn, circled in dark bracken, lording the land, the watchful eternal eye. He too would be a witness. The cold northerly wind gusted off the Loch, a stark reminder of the live earth, whispering nothings. It had snowed a little during the night, a sprinkling, powdered sugar to celebrate his coming. He felt joyous at the simplicity of the land and nature. No worrisome thoughts, no conflict, just being at one with the earth, the birds, the many noises and scents coming from the forest behind. Snaps of wood, shuffles, squalls and squeals. It all came alive to rejoice in life and death. Passengers to accompany him on his quest. They too would be witnesses.

Then he thought, who is he in this land? An intruder, a source of boding calamity, a sort of anti-Christ of nature or, as he wanted to believe, part of it. An integral part of the forest, mountains, animals and noises. He was the wind; he was the forest; he was nature incarnate. The pinnacle of existence. A human being. A human being, a strange concept in our modern world where existence and worth are reduced to performance or failure. To be a human is by far not enough. Yet, exulting, we can be, to exist, to think... to act. To act? Hm. He pondered the fallen wood, then bent to gather it up onto the pile against the cabin. An act, albeit small, can change everything. Who was he to act? He was the thinker. The lost thinker. Erring blindly along a cliff's edge. But to act! Now there's an interesting thing.

He was just leaning the rake against the cabin when a reddish glint pulled his attention to the lakeside, not twenty yards away. There, proud in a sideways stance, showing his full stature, bushy tail erect and green intelligent eyes drilling into his, stood a fox. John froze, not wanting to startle the animal, then admired the beauty of something estranged to the meddling of men. The pure essence of life, a totem of hope and innocence. The fox was stoic yet had one clipped ear, taken in a fight perhaps. It was quizzing him, sizing him up, measuring the creature before it: a human being. As the fox continued to watch him, John had a sense of existence. He existed! The fox was looking at him. He meant something to it; it was significant.

John moved first with one small slow step. The fox skittered away along the Loch with a slight limp, then turned into the forest, gone. John smiled inwardly and outwardly. A triumphant smile of birth and being. He stood there for a few minutes, gulping the waters of salvation. Rejuvenating. Purifying. He sensed, seemingly for the first time in his life, the meaning of self, reflected in the fox's eyes. An apocalypse for the artificial scaffold of life. His heart thrown asunder, strewn across the land of desolation, trodden in the earth, buried even, to satiate that very quintessence of existence, so rare and elusive. Yes, his heart was his and could be called back like a faithful sheep dog to lap the love of his master. He hailed his heart. It came back with a thump! He stooped, crippled in tears, sobbing, crying, yelling until, many minutes later, exhaustion led him to unconsciousness, a land of peace and rebirth.

Chapter 6

"Hello, beautiful animal"

Consciousness came, little by little, like the first raindrops heralding a storm. He sensed not his body, only his cheek glued to the frozen ground, numb yet throbbing. His members were notions of memories, an inkling of self. He felt a rasp against his cheek, the one facing the sky, wet, yet warm. He was not alone. He opened one eye, the one not held to ground.

Two large green eyes stared at him not twelve inches away. A long red snout nudged his tear stricken face, urging him to life. His heart rampaged, pumping sensation and life into his body. He moved one hand and pushed sideways to roll over and pull his face from the cold ground. With both eyes, he stared at the creature before him. It was the fox, the same as before with the clipped ear. It came back, looking at him with intent, not scared, a companion. He felt it immediately.

He felt dizzy as awareness welled up inside him. One after another things came into focus, both mentally and physically. The fox stood there, expectant.

"Hello, beautiful animal," John whispered. He sat there, not waiting for a reply but sharing existence with such purity, so much truth held within innocence. He sighed deeply with sublime satisfaction. Tears of joy rolled down his sodden cheeks, cleansing, cleansing.

The fox, who had been standing, sat, its tongue halfway out of its snout.

John smiled at it and it smiled back.

"Are you not scared of me?" said John, prepared for a monologue of expiation.

"Now why would I be scared of you?" said the fox.

John let slip the hand holding him up. "Did you just speak?" he wondered aloud.

"Indeed, I did. I like a friendly chat every now and again. Its healthy," said the fox with a flapping of its tongue.

John shook his head. Was he going mad? Is this what happens when you lose touch with reality? When society shuns you, making you retreat into the darkness and obscure depths of the mind. He struggled to get up and fell down twice on the hard ground.

"Take is easy, you were out for some time. Your limbs are sure stiff and heart stricken. Crawl on all fours. Like me, it's easier. Go inside and warm up."

"You're full of advice for a fox, aren't you? What do you care? And anyway... I need to suffer, to feel the raw anguish of my soul. I need to feel alive. Yet, here I am talking to a fox. I failed."

"Failed not my friend and why suffer? The realisation of what or who you are is a time of celebration. Look at me. I am a fox. I live in the forest and forage to find food. Sometimes I gander on the hills basking in the sun, sometimes I slumber in the warm embrace of my love. I know who I am. Do you? I wonder."

He shivered; his nerves waking up, calling his body to act, to move. "I must get warm. I need to go inside. Will you come?"

"No, inside? No, my place is here, in the wild. But I will come back later. I have some things to look after. I'll come back when you call me."

"How do I call you?"

"That, my friend, is the art of it all. Learn," the fox saw movement in the forest. "Must be off. See you later." He trotted off into the forest, leaving John bewildered and bemused.

He made the door to the cabin on all fours, opened it and crawled in. A couple of logs on the dying embers, a blanket over his shoulder and a coffee from the pot he'd made earlier, he sat on a chair not two feet away from the reviving fire. The warmth and light, a balsam to his heart. His heart, he'd called it back. It came and struck him. What did that mean? How did he feel now? He felt… entire, as though something was missing before. His soul satiated with the secure feeling of being one. A feeling he had not had for a long time. Something was missing before, absent, lost or forgotten. He did not know. But now, looking into the fire, he saw his image reflected by the shapes of the flames as though it were mirroring him, calling out to him. He felt good as the heat permeated his body and relaxed his muscles. The fox? Talking to a fox, well, that was new. Was it a part of him, sharing in his predicament. No. He'd said he had a good life in the wild, free to amble wherever his desires took him. No ties, no responsibilities, no obedience's, no following. Following? Was he a follower, striving to keep up with the rest, with the world? Always a step late, a step back, forever overshadowed. Yet was he what he wanted the world to be? Certainly not up to now. Suffering the iniquities of this system, everybody's fears and phantasmagorical ideas of persecution and strife. The illusional monsters of the Id that most people nurtured like a pet cat, thriving off the victim status the world encouraged. All to divide and rule. All lost on their separate islands, lost in the magma of humanity, in the spiralling call to be noticed and accepted. A race from womb to grave. Always taking part, never winning.

Then how to exist in such a society? How to grow in stature. His father used to say: Be bigger than the problem. Good counsel, but how when faced with blind fear and ignorance? How to overcome the lowly thinking with love and grandeur?

He needed to talk to the fox again. But first, sleep. He felt emptied, a barrel scraped clean and blasted with fire to eradicate any final, lingering residues of doubt and dread. He headed for his bed, buried himself in blankets and slept peacefully.

Chapter 6

Heart to heart

He rose in the afternoon. No idea what time it was, but invigorated by a sleep he'd never had before. So sound, so still, so peaceful. He couldn't recollect a dream or having fidgeted. He woke in the same position as he had when he went under. A sleep so renewing, blissful. He felt himself, the same, yet different. He touched all the parts of his body, feeling his skin, his toes, his genitals. All was so real, so present and... existing. Existing for him. It was him, his body, his capsule of life. His thoughts sauntered through his mind. A garden in clear sunlight. Paths leading to unseen wonders hidden behind shrubberies and cool shadows. A garden to discover, to play and celebrate life. He took in a deep breath, drew some fresh coffee and decided to eat out tonight. A fire between the loch and the cabin, a log to sit against and something to grill. Late afternoon in January invited the shadows and obscurity. He didn't mind. The world was his, he would light it up with the wellbeing of entirety. A whole, complete. Yet, questions sizzled in his mind. To find peace with himself is one thing, to find peace with our surroundings is another. He thought about his family, the office, the pub. The people he saw, astray, lost and empty, ignorant of their plight, drinking the insomnious lies and believing the charade.

* * *

He bought wood from the side of the cabin, some small wood too to start the fire, and gave life to a warming core of benevolence, cracking and spitting into activity. Clad in warm clothes, a bottle of wine grounded into the needles next to the log and the tray of sausages and corn cobs, he settled down, bathing in the warmth. As dusk fell, the blue sky gradually became a pure pink. The Loch was still, a grey, pink vista of quiet contemplation. He felt at peace nestled between the log and the fire. The forest, it's presence, a welcome friend. He felt sure that Rois-Bheinn too was looking on with approval. A witness to the birth of a man.

After a few sips of wine and placing a couple of cobs onto the small grill hung over the fire, he expired with joy. The beauty of this place, nature, alone and the kindness of the land invaded his senses, his heart. Love. Love of things. What a programme, he thought. What a challenge. But how to love all things?

He heard a shuffle in the needles not far and saw the Fox approach, slowly, carefully, eyeing the fire. Its green eyes reflecting the red fire, two sentinels watching, curious and friendly.

 "Hello Fox."

"Glad to see you're all right."

"I slept."

"Good, you needed it. You don't lose and get back your heart every day."

"No. It struck me hard. But oh, how I feel now. So much better. Like it was missing all the time," John said, placing a couple of sausages onto the grill.

"Perhaps it was. May I ask you a question?" said the fox, eyeing the sausages.

"Off course, what can be more normal than a fox wanting to ask a question?"

"Everyone has a heart," the fox said, ignoring the kind sarcasm, "Some use it badly, selfishly, some are led by it. Worse, some, and perhaps most, ignore it. How is your heart?" said the fox, licking the saliva drooling from its jowls.

John thought for a moment, supped some wine, and then answered, "I am so thirsty for love. There is little in this world. I hunger for a meaningful life, to get it and to provide it. To live and contribute to a world without malice. It that asking too much?"

"Noble, but naïve. Why would you want that?"

"Why what? To live in a world without malice?"

"Yes."

"I…," he thought for a moment, "Because I feel no malice in me."

"And you think that is the way for everyone?" John could swear the fox was smirking.

"Well, no, of course not. But at least lean toward kindness, favour forgiveness, and build meaning in people's lives. There is too much destruction on a physical and social level. It's the way of the world. I don't think it has to be that way."

"So true. You know that most people are not kind and open. They are victims of their desires if they are not victims of others. Would you love someone who is bad?"

"Do I have to love them?"

"Well, if you want to change the world, good idea by the way, you'll need to rise above those things. Be bigger."

"That'll be hard. How?"

"Before we go on, those things you put on the grill smell lovely. Can I have one? Please," the fox grinned.

"Of course," he took one off and laid it on the log, "Wait for it to cool down. It's hot."

"Do you think there is a reason for everything?" the fox said, slowly approaching the sausage.

"Hmm, not everything, accidents and stuff like that. But I think people's actions or reactions are nearly all down to what they think or believe."

"That's what I meant. But you cannot possibly know their reasoning, the why of things."

"No," John said, "But to use insight and kindness will go a long way to forgiving and mending. If I can only control my emotions."

The fox made for the sausage and bit into it, "Lovely," it said between gulps.

"Ah yes, our famous pork sausages," he took one himself, on the end of a stick.

They chewed in companionable silence for a moment.

"This is so strange, yet so meaningful. Chatting to a fox. I like you fox. You are good. Thank you for your company."

"My pleasure. So, emotions... why would you want to control them? Don't you think they have a use?"

"Indeed, they do, but most are controlled by them rather than the other way. It hurts to see it. It hurts me when I fail."

"I understand. Is that why you want to control them? To no longer feel the pain of error?"

"Yes, I need to read me more honestly than I have previously. I want my heart to shine, to care and savour the good side of people."

"Why is that important to you John?"

"How did you know my name?"

"Oh, you know, wily and cunning, that's me. I know things like that. Don't worry. So why?"

"What? Oh... yes, I feel that love is so abundant in each one of us, yet disregarded somehow. People are embarrassed to talk about it or rarely express their feelings on the subject. It's all superficial. Some depth in our relations would go far to heal our sores."

They talked and talked till late and the sausages ran out. John was in osmosis with the fox. It felt so strange to have such openness from someone, even a fox. It felt so good, wholesome and natural.

Perhaps, a thought came to him, it was his revived heart embracing the fox's friendship. His capacity to love. No reasoning, no questioning, just acceptance of the reality of his mind. A kind of purposeful reality, virtuous. He wanted to hold on to that reality, his. And share. Sleep welcomed him to its compassionate approval, reconciliation between mind and heart. The healing of a hurt Bushi.

The ideals which have lighted my way, and time after time have given me new courage to face life cheerfully, have been Kindness, Beauty and Truth.

Albert Einstein, 1954

Chapter 7

"Thank you fox"

He rose the next morning, sprite, clear and purposeful. He immediately went to the window looking onto the loch, nurturing a vain hope to see the fox. It was not there.

Later, after stocking the stove, a wash and some biscuits with a coffee, he went out to inspect their hearth of reconciliation. It was as he left it. He looked up to Rois-Bheinn, proud, unmoving, gleaming in the morning sun, and gave a nod of shared respect. "Thank you, mountain."

He moved up to the water's edge, knelt, cupped a hand in the cold murky waters and held out his hand to the sky, the water running down his arm in its chilly envelopment. "Thank you, water."

He then turned toward the forest, ever present, ever watching. He bowed and said, "Thank you, forest."

He then spun around and around crying at the top of his voice, "Thank you, Thank you, Thank you," rejoicing to be amid love and faithfulness.

Then he knelt on the ground, crying in joy and said, "Thank you fox, thank you. I shall miss you wherever you are."

A voice, galactic, yet within, said, "Never shall you miss me. I love you as you have shown love to me. Go to the world and rejoice in life and all its potential. We are as one."

A US Space Force Novella

Semper Supra

Mike Lees

Chapter 1

Space, quite close to us

Admiral Am'trach proudly stood on the bridge of the Nor'tilous, the Super Dreadnaught, Flagship of the Cerulean fleet, as it swam through the black toward their next undertaking. His fleet had travelled through space for several months now, and the Captains on the other ships were reporting increasing unrest among the crews. It was time, time to conquer, to bleed and taste the inebriating joys of battle and drink the lusty blood of their enemies. He too was thirsty, greed to engage and decimate, to pillage and kill. This was their destiny and their life. To roam the spiral arm and seek the weak, to annihilate and stand upon the shores of the defeated. He licked his lips in anticipation.

Yet, time was telling, the high of their last engagement, a long lost luscious memory, was no longer able to fuel the hatred and anger that became each mighty warrior within their ranks. They needed something, and soon. He needed it too, like he needed air to breathe.

His thoughts were interrupted by the sensor operator, "Admiral, Sir, I have a reading coming up on our starboard side. We have arrived at the target system, Sir. It has eight planets, one of which looks promising."

"Show me."

Am'trach approached the screen and gave a sigh of satisfaction, "At last. That third planet has certainly living creatures, a civilisation if we are lucky. Very well," he turned to the navigation officer, "Plot a course for that planet Mr Zu'lou, and inform me how long it will take. I will be in my stateroom," then he turned to the communications officer, "Inform Captain Ha'dok of our course change," he said as he marched off the Bridge toward his room.

Several moments later Mr Zu'lou informed him it would take three days to reach the planet. Am'trach rubbed his hands in delight. At last, blood and battle! He thought to himself, not with a certain glee. Yet the Consortium of Governments plead for a more peaceful solution to civilisations who represent, or may soon, a risk to the Spiral Arm they were overseeing. More so to protect their hold on the systems within. Damn, he will have to conform and seek a solution. But maybe this new planet will give him rise to deploy his forces of destruction. If they were lucky.

The days passed quickly while the fleet was bubbling over in excitement and preparations. During that time, they also cumulated an impressive intelligence package on the civilisation living on the planet. The inhabitants called it Earth. A thorough evaluation of the enemies' capabilities, both civil and military, were established and issued to all Captains of the

Fleet, who then provided this intelligence to their divisions and services with the required deployment parameters. Primary, secondary and tertiary targets chosen and allotted to the corresponding fleet arms for execution upon the orders of the Admiral. The Cerulean fleet was poised to inflict total annihilation, swift, bloody and glorifying. The mood within the fleet was ecstatic, the preparations tactically perfect. Only the Admiral knew he'd have to use a bit of reserve.

Am'trach perused the readiness, and intelligence reports flowing into his office with deep, cold satisfaction. He felt the energy within his ship, the thirst to enter a challenge, eager to scorn the bloodied bodies of their enemy. His day of complete victory and eternity came to bear. This will be his defining moment, the summit of his career; he will be a god among his people for eternity, a resounding victory to emulate the Cerulean people throughout the galaxy. No longer will we be a mockery of the other spiral arms. They will learn to respect us.

Chapter 2

Weekend washout

President Peter Walters, using a moment of calm and solitude in his office, laid his head in his hands to quell a fresh bout of fitful panic. His suit felt tight, damp and clinging as he heaved to fill his lungs. His warm hands a welcome balm to his tired eyes and worn soul. He was in the middle of his term and wondered how he made it that far without caving in. His age and the never-ending demands of his administration seemed to devour him. He hardly made any press conferences and avoided where possible any public addresses. Although the former was becoming more and more difficult to avoid, despite having the mainstream press on his side who were doing their utmost to bolster his image and cover up his failing health and mental awareness. But there were limits to everything. The Senate and the Congress made increasing calls for more transparency and reliable information. They wanted a Commander-in-Chief present, able and strong. He was none of them. He was even getting flak from members of his own party. Another two years of this, he thought. He shuddered and let loose a tear. He should resign, his vice-president could take the reins. She was handling most of the stuff anyway, thank god. Both domestic and foreign. His image in the world was lamentable, and domestic tensions were growing by the day. He didn't know how to handle most situations and relied heavily on his administration. Still, he made it, at last, President of the USA, after years of political fighting with meagre results, he made it. The most powerful man on this planet, some would say. He sighed inwardly. At least no major catastrophes have arisen, and perhaps he might just make it to the end. He felt tired and threadbare, muddled. An aide entered his office, Interrupting his train of thought, "Yes, James?" he said, looking up with red eyes adjusting to the light. James knew better than to stare. "My helicopter ready?"

"Sir, your weekend at Camp David may have to wait…."

Walter's shoulders visibly slumped. *What now?* He thought to himself.

"We have an urgent call in from General George Bastion at Peterson," he said, trying to keep his tone light.

"Peterson? Oh, the air force base, yes?"

"It's the Peterson Space Force Base, Sir. You inaugurated the new designation five months ago here in the Whitehouse naming General Bastion in charge of the facility. He requests to talk to you immediately. We have our administration's team of military advisors and consultants listening in, as well as General Branston from the Pentagon and his team. Shall I put him through on line three?" James said.

"Yes, go ahead."

"Mr President, General Bastion here from Peterson. How are you today?"

"Excellent George, and how's it over in Ohio?"

"We're in Colorado, Peter."

"Exact. James here tells me you have an urgent matter. What gives?"

"Well, Peterson makes continual deep space scans-"

"Of course," Walters interrupted.

"… and one of our satellites around the Moon, has detected a series of faint but distinct readings coming in from a thirty-degree angle above the plane of our solar system."

"Meteorite shower?"

"At first, that is what we thought, but further readings from other satellites gave us a three-dimensional image of what we're now calling the Swarm. We're picking up signals moving in formation Sir…" the General let that sink in.

"Formation? What does that mean George?" Peter could feel his throat tightening.

"It means what it means. A formation. It's not natural. A meteorite shower would be haphazard. This is not. As this anomaly gets nearer, we'll get a better picture, but the formation is real and has raised concerns and speculation here at Peterson. Especially that this Swarm is moving straight for us. Estimated time of arrival is six hours, Sir. I would strongly suggest you implementing at least DEFCON 3. I need this base to be ready and our units prepped. As we operate in space, I need to go ahead now, sir. We have little time and our units need all they can get to initiate launch procedures."

"Yes, I understand. But try not to fret too much. This may be nothing. I will consult with my team here. Please send all the data you have now and we'll get back to you. Thank you, George."

"Be hasty, Peter. I have a feeling about this."

"We will, George. We will. Thank you." Walter placed the phone down. *Damn, what's this all about? Just when he needed a break at Camp David and now this*. He thought to himself.

"Sir, shall I usher in our military reps and science teams?"

He'd completely forgotten James was still in his office. "Eh, yes, of course. Let's see what they think of this."

Moments later his office was filled to the brim with several military liaison officers, a batch of scientific advisors and several aides and political representatives, most of whom were consulting their laptops on the fly.

Walters leaned back into his chair and let out an audible sigh. "Ok everybody, what do we have?"

"Absolutely fascinating, Sir," said Williamson, the Head of the Whitehouse scientific team, as he moved towards Walters' desk. "These images require more study and evaluation, but from first sight their trajectory and formation suggest something other than natural," he finished, relieved he found a sentence without using the word Alien.

"Fine, but what can we expect from this information, what can we deduce? Are we in danger? Is there a risk?" Walters asked to the group of people in front of him.

"I for one would put us on maximum alert, at least DEFCON 2. They'll be here in six hours. They're fast," said General Carters, chief military attaché to the Whitehouse.

At that moment, Joanne Blaze, the Vice-President, came in commanding everyone's attention. "I have seen the images and spectrum analysis and concur that a DEFCON 2 is advisable," she said, looking directly at Walters. "The information we have is insufficient to define the risk but we should be on the alert, DEFCON 2 gives us a response time concurrent with the expected ETA of those objects. I have ordered our Foreign dept. to contact their counterparts in Russia and China to verify this information with them and to ensure that neither is involved. For now, we are unable to establish that," she finished and sat down on the couch.

Walters was awash with incertitude. If his order to go to DEFCON 2 proved unnecessary, he would have the Senate and the Congress on his back, without what the media would make of it. Damn, why now? Why me? Then he thought perhaps he can delay the decision, wait to see if there is a real danger before alerting the Military and more important, putting his career at risk and loosing face with his peers. How could he be blamed when no intelligence can show at this moment that a risk is involved? No, sit tight, ride it out. And perhaps that weekend at Camp David would still be on. "Thank you, Joanne. I understand your concern, however, I believe the best course for us would be to gather more detailed information about this event prior to making any hasty decisions which we might regret later," Walters said, resisting an urge to rub his temples. He turned his attention to M. Williamson, "Please gather as much information as possible from the data sent to us by Peterson and any updates. I want a report in my office in thirty minutes. You may go," he said, looking down at his desk, feigning a deep interest in a bit of paper.

Chapter 3

Space, closer

"Four hours to orbit, Sir, we are commencing retro feeds now," informed the sensor operator, unable to hide his excitement.

"Very well. Pass me Mr Zu'lou."

"Admiral, Zu'lou at your command, sir."

"Good, arrange a comm call with all the fleet's captains in ten minutes, please," he cut off the communication.

He admired the vids on his wall showing multiple views of his fleet, his Flagship, a Super Dreadnaught, the twenty accompanying standard Dreadnaught class ships, ninety-seven battleships, sixty frigates and finally the huge carriers, one hundred and twenty in all. Packed with fighters, land assault vehicles and troop carriers. They carried four hundred thousand troops, highly trained and equipped. It was a war Machine devoted to one aim: kill for the emulation and ultimate domination of the Cerulean people in the Galaxy. That was his view anyway.

"Admiral, Sir, in ten seconds."

Ten seconds to glory.

A red light showed up on his desk microphone…

"Captains of the Cerulean Fleet. Our people have vested in us the responsibility to emulate the grandeur of our race in the Galaxy. We have been assigned a task beyond what normal beings can imagine. Our glory will be in the history books for time immemorial. We shall rise to the forefront of not only this allotted spiral arm, but the entire Galaxy. Our allies and enemies will look upon us as the grandest and courageous fighting force ever to be assembled and will strike terror and admiration amongst those who peruse our endeavours," he paused and coughed for effect, "We are nearing our next and probably the most difficult task set before us. That planet below represents for us the deployment and culmination of all the might and technological expertise our race possesses, and we shall be victorious. We will trample upon the bodies of this enemy who deign to venture into the realms of space without the slightest idea of what is out there. They are foolhardy, naïve, and nurture a place of choice within our galactic community. I tell you today that that will not happen. We shall quell any calculations they have of greatness and adventure. They shall realise that the Galaxy is not theirs to play with and that we will tolerate no attempt of conquering our spiral. Today, my friends, we go into glory, into eternity."

He clicked off the microphone and took a deep breath. Indeed, this was it, this was his moment in history. Activating the microphone again, he called M Zu'lou, "M Zu'lou, please convene a meeting with

Captain Ha'dok and the chief officers, in my private meeting room immediately. Tell them I want a review of intelligence so far collated regarding out next objective. Thank you."

Several moments later, he could hear scurrying and hushed voices in the corridor as the Officers filed into the meeting room next to his stator-room. Good, the chief officers are keen to meet and discuss our next victory. He thought to himself with satisfaction.

The meeting room was full, although not crowded. It was well appointed and designed to receive the full contingent of officers on board the flagship. Everyone was talking in low voices, even whispers, that stopped when Admiral Am'Trach strode in, went directly to the head of the long table, and took his seat.

"Greetings ladies and gentlemen, I want a full review of this Earth, as the inhabitants call it. What do you have? Captain Ha'dok, please start."

The Captain had a wad of paper in front of him but held the Admiral's stare with bright blue eyes and a stern look. "Preliminary scans show a race technologically well into the second period of advancement our race had several generations ago. While they have been into space, only crude fossil fuel rockets are used and though many died during their first incursions off planet they have persisted and have established one space station which purportedly houses five people at the moment."

"Purportedly?" asked the Admiral.

"Indeed, we have analysed the videos feeds they are sending to Earth and distributing to the public. They are fake. We have discussed this anomaly between us before this meeting and can only deduce that this is to generate popularity among the population and gain a high status in the eyes of the Government.

All to ensure funding is kept at its present level. The same can be said for their announced moon landings, all of which were fabricated. The reasons were elsewhere, the Americans, a country accepted widely as a leading power between the elites, were in a tight struggle with another country, Russia. To beat them, they faked the landings. Of course, this goes beyond our comprehension and shows the state this human race is in. Regarding the space station, it is primitive and subject to damage from meteors and wears badly under the harsh radiation their sun is emitting. However, they have cumulated a vast array of satellites of various designs and purposes. All of which are rudimentary in design and subject to failure because of either mechanical or computer weaknesses."

"Do any of them have a defensive purpose?" asked the Admiral looking directly at the Captain.

Without blinking or showing any signs of wavering, the Captain said, "Not to our knowledge. They are all surveillance and communication related."

"And their earth based weapons?"

The Captain smiled, "They are all of a ballistic nature, Sir. They have no quantum lasers nor ionizers. However, they are doing deep research into those fields and may, one day, develop something akin to our own weaponry. As I say, they do not have that technology. They do, however, have nuclear power which was used against their own people."

"By the Great Spirit of Anon! All the more reason we intervene. I think we came just in time," the Admiral added.

"Indeed, Sir, Lieutenant Lilash Fl'rt has further information from an anthropological and social point of view. Lieutenant, please," the Captain said, looking over the table to a beautiful female smartly dressed in her black and gold uniform.

"Thank you Sir," she then turned to the Admiral, "Sir, they call themselves Humans. Their known history goes back to around ten thousand of their sun cycles. But only during the last two hundred have they made enormous strides technologically, mainly because of greed and power by a few. Their first and well-documented attempt at industrialisation of craftsmanship was a Machine designed to comb cotton, a plant used to make clothes. They had people working for them in 'Factories', making them work 86 percent of their time to a Master who gave them in return meagre sustenance to survive. This model grew to a system today where you could say 98 percent of the population are in subservience to the Elites. With a technologically based society, the Elites have cemented their hold on the individual whom they have isolated from others in a devious system called addresses and identity. Data on who they are and where they live. Everyone is isolated, when dealing with the Elites. This enables them to take action against any one individual who does not comply. Communities of people do not exist or are hindered, if not outlawed, except in remote lands where they have no interest. Through lies and deceit, laws and manipulation they control and dictate the people's actions, limit their possessions and it would appear, more and more so, control an individual's way of thinking, with an exponential punishment system. The Elites also have a system in place to take wealth from the people to further their own prosperity and stature. It has got to a point that the Elite will always keep power and wealth while different mechanisms, which ensure their obedience, keeps the majority in place, sometimes if only to survive and avoid punishment. The status quo is strengthened as time goes by. The Humans are not free people like we enjoy back home. Their role in society is already ordained at birth. Meaning the financial profile or heritage of a person is determinant. Law forces the majority to learn basic skills at school, then an exploitable skill later. After which they seek to sign off their lives to work for a Master until they can no longer function because of ill health and old age." Everyone pushed sighs of horror at hearing this, hushed comments flew around the room.

Second lieutenant, M Sh'ish said, "That seems awful, how can they tolerate being treated like that?"

"From what I can gather from their literature, media and laws, conditioning is accepted from birth. At only four eightieths of their lives, hardly weaned from their mothers, they are put into a system to condition their minds. They call it kindergarten and later school. When they reach adult age and after their formatting, they are subject to liminal, subliminal, conscious and subconscious coercion to believe such a course is a valued aim. I know, it seems horrifying, but the Elite feed them lies so they think their lives mean something and obedience to the system in place is a good thing. The subjugated avoid going against their leaders or masters to escape punishment. Some are free thinkers and attempt to struggle free from the model set before them, but they are quickly and efficiently marginalised and ridiculed by the Elite, media and various social constructs. Others are outright persecuted and killed."

"Thank you, lieutenant Fl'rt for your precious insight. Indeed, their society is disturbing. I have another question for you, Lieutenant. Do they know what war is?"

"Indeed, they do. Their history is full of conflicts, conquering and colonisation. Recently they had what they called two World Wars which were decided upon by different parties of the Elites."

"And who fought these wars?" asked the Admiral.

"The lower classes were conditioned early on to sacrifice their own lives to save the Elites systems of exploitation and domination. Millions died during those two wars, while smaller local wars still go on and mainly because of the same reasons. The Elites seek to secure their power over the people and have installed an institution called the United Nations, to emulate their own local system although they keep, each one, their own sovereignty on certain subjects when it suites them. On an economic front, they created a group called the G7, so the Elites could cartelise their exploitation within their respective regions and spheres of influence and harmonize their structures to inhibit anyone wishing to escape by a system called Border and immigration Control and for possessions, Customs. If you want to move possessions to one system of Elites to another, they will take money from you, failing which they will seize your possessions. Some Elites, or States, have isolated themselves from the rest, if only to exploit more severely their own people. Their world is divided, and mistrust is the standby for many of them."

"Amazing," said the Admiral, "how can such a race survive with such a system of self-denial? It almost seems fictional. I think we are doing their race a favour to dismantle their present system and curtail their yearnings to go into space. Imagine if we have that sort of mentality roaming the Galaxy? It would be disastrous," the Admiral finished with a shudder. Everyone around the table agreed with comments of disbelief.

"And religion?" asked M Sh'ish. Everyone turned again to Lieutenant Fl'rt.

"They tolerate religion, inasmuch that it does not interfere with the economic consolidation and their control over individuals. Most States and institutions dismiss any belief in a higher entity and minimise its import against the benefits of obeying them and giving over their earnings through what they call taxes and forced consumption. In order to counter religion in favour of politically biased scientific overviews, they distil the following dogma: That they exist from nothing, they call it evolution." She looked around the table, trying to hold back a smirk.

"Unbelievable," whispered the Admiral.

"Indeed, so, but anyone who wants to remain in their favour pay reverence to that story. Otherwise, they are banished, ridiculed or cancelled, as they are presently calling it."

The Admiral shifted in his seat, disturbed by the news, "So, if I understand correctly, most of the humans are enslaved to the Elite's system?" he looked around the table, making sure he made eye contact with everyone present, "Despite myself, it would be inappropriate to condemn so many humans who are ignorant of the big picture. What are your suggestions as we approach this planet?"

Silence fell onto the meeting, those quietly exchanging with their neighbours quietened and looked up. Others shuffled paper in front of them. Then Lieutenant Fl'rt coughed and raised her hand, "In view of the radical and rampant infighting this race is experiencing, it will be a long time before they attain any level of technology to endanger our spiral. If we do nothing, they will, one day attain their goals and in view of their duplicitous manner of handing things will not be viable partners with other races under our auspices."

"So, what do you suggest, Lieutenant?" said the Admiral.

"It may not be the complete victory we were looking for, but an EMP strike would cripple the Elites system of slavery and enable everyone to return to a more natural way of life. Individuals could express themselves freely and perhaps lessons would be learnt, but the latter is not guaranteed. An EMP would immediately affect their technological infrastructure. Their system is highly reliant on electricity. Machines, communications, media, transport, etc. They would revert to a time about two hundred years in the past. As they have largely digitalised their history and knowledge, much of that will be lost. They would be harmless for centuries to come," she looked around the room with a sigh, "As for our image in the spiral, it would show our magnanimity toward a race most of whom are innocent and coerced. An EMP strike would hurt the Elites the most, although much damage and strife will ensue for the population who have been led to depend on the system."

"Thank you, Lieutenant. Any other suggestions?" He looked around the table.

Major Ax'e looked up with a stern face, "I say we go ahead with the annihilation. We have no guarantee that they will not pose a threat to the Spiral in the future. It's what we do, anyway."

"Indeed, so," said M. Sm'if, the diplomatic attaché to the fleet, "And I for one would understand that course of action. However, the Lieutenant's remark concerning our image to the other races within this spiral has merit. We all know that we are striving to attain an influential position within the Spiral arm and perhaps, later, on a Galactic scale. To do so, I believe simple war and destruction would not serve our long-term goals. More so to the contrary. If we can show forbearance and magnanimity to this race, it may well be in our favour. After all, military prowess is not the only language the Central Core understands. Disruption of the Human's present wayward activities by an EMP would enhance our image and contribute to the mature, level minded, approach our Emperor adheres to."

Damn him, thought the Admiral, he is right though. I have to adopt the long view here.

"Very well ladies and gentlemen, we shall adjourn this meeting for reflection. Captain Ha'dok, please put our fleet in a holding position pending our decision. I will convene another meeting soon to decide upon our actions. Thank you all. You are dismissed."

They took the decision to move to orbit a short time later, given that no immediate and obvious danger confronted the fleet. An EMP strike would be enabled at the earliest possible time. The Fleet surged on.

Chapter 4

Swarm?

James knocked on the President's door and entered, "Sir, M Williamson and two members of his team are here to review the present situation with the eh… event. General Carters and two aides are also waiting outside with updates."

"Please show them in James and thank you," Walters said, unable to hide the weariness tugging him down into his seat.

After everyone had filed in, laptops at the ready, Walters invited them to sit on the couches, more so to have a comfortable seat than any political game setting. "Williamson, what do you have?" he said finally, after they served coffee.

"Indeed, we have clearer pictures of the swarm," he looked over to the President, "It looks rather impressive," said Williamson, looking down to his screen.

"Swarm?" asked the President, "How many of them are there?"

"We estimate approximately three hundred units. They are very faint as they are still far out, but we are getting some trails, perhaps exhaust fumes of matter residue. As for the formation, although quite elegant, doesn't tell me anything," he said looking over to the General.

"Sir, in the last twenty minutes they have rearranged their ships into what our military might call an attack formation. Some signals are stronger than others, that suggest larger craft, and in the centre of the formation. There are two groups which have split up on either side of the swarm, no doubt to stave off any flank attack."

"So you believe this is a concerted incursion into our system with military goals?" asked Walters.

At that moment the Vice-President came swanning in and took a seat next to the President. "Sorry for being late, I was on a call to both Russia and China. This is new to them and they are evaluating the situation as we speak."

"Thank you, Mrs Blaze. General, please continue."

"Indeed, I do. To answer your question. This is no natural phenomenon, we need to take this seriously. However-"

The President cut in, "What do we have to counter this threat, if it is a threat?"

"We are considering this a threat. We need DEFCON 2 to get our units into space. Although, due to budget restrictions and other deemed priorities, our means are limited."

"What do you mean, General?"

"We have two secret shuttles which we can get into space within three hours. Aboard those vessels, we will have two teams of Space Guardians trained for combat in space, placing explosives and/or boarding vessels in vacuum. However, the Shuttles themselves have no weapons and would be quite ineffective if the Swarm were to be hostile."

"That's all we have?"

"Not entirely, we can get some missiles up into space that can lock onto given targets but only within a short range from earth. We would have to wait for them to enter orbit to launch an attack. We don't really know what we are up against. If they are aliens," he looked over to Williamson with a smirk, "There capability should be superior to ours although we know nothing at the moment."

"So, in reality, we are completely unprepared for this and what we have is like pissing against a storm?"

"Something like that, Sir."

"M Williamson, any ideas on their capabilities?" said the President taking a sip of his coffee.

"Well, to get here in such large numbers suggests ample resources and knowhow and certainly advance technology. When and if they get into orbit, we'll be able to study them better, but then it might be too late. Apart from that, we do not know their means at disposal nor their intentions. Which leads us-"

"Sir," interrupted Blaze looking to the President, "I would strongly suggest we go to DEFCON 2. We will advise our friends, the Chinese and Russians of the reason we do that. I would also suggest we try to contact the eh… aliens. We may get a better hold on what they are trying to do.”

Walters needed time to think, but time was short and the pressure was building up. “Very well. General, please initiate DEFCON 2 and get those units up into space,” he then craned his neck to look at Mrs Blaze, “Please get M Cortez in, we need a diplomatic approach,” then he eyed General Carters, “How do we contact them?”

“The ISS is the obvious choice. Their signals are clear of our atmosphere; so long-range communications should be optimal. They would then relay the communication, if one were to be established, with us at Peterson who would then set-up a call with you Sir.”

“Good, make it happen, General. That is all. James? Please let M. Cortez in as soon as he is here. Thank you.”

Everybody filed out except Mrs Blaze, who followed the President up to his desk and sat opposite, "You're doing very well, Peter. Do nothing rash, ok?" she said a bit too sternly.

"Yes mother," he said jokingly then looked pensive, "Do we really have a Space Force?"

"Indeed, we do, albeit, limited in its capacities, they will get a better hold on what we are up against than anyone ground based."

M Cortez entered the Office. "Good afternoon Sir, Mrs Blaze," he nodded, "What can I do for you?"

"Take a seat, coffee?"

"Thank you and no thank you. I just had one. So what is this all about? I saw General Carters and M. Williamson rush down the corridors, hung on their phones and trailed by their people. They seemed stressed."

"Indeed, they should be," Walters stared at M Cortez a bit too long, making the latter feel uneasy. "M Cortez, I believe you wrote a pamphlet on First Contact Protocols. Is that right?"

"Yes Sir, it was just a tentative sketch. More science fiction than anything else, although I gave a reality edge to it, which made it plausible. Why?" he looked from Walters to Blaze, wondering what this was all about.

"Joanne, please inform M Cortez."

"Inform me of what?" he said, looking toward Mrs Blaze.

"Two hours ago we got a call from our facility in Colorado, Peterson Space Force base. They informed us of a certain number of 'objects' coming toward earth, in formation," she lay emphasis on the last word, "They will arrive here in well less than six hours. We believe they are of alien origin and estimate at least three hundred objects or vessels. We want to talk to them," she finished, leaving the words hang in the air.

Cortez was caught up in internal thoughts for a moment before realising where he was, "Sorry, I was thinking about something. That is incredible. Fantastic as well. How can I help?"

"Given the situation, what would be the best approach if we were to acquire communications with them?"

Cortez looked into infinity for a second, "If the communication is just verbal, then the language will certainly be a problem. With visuals, you can convey much more. Facial expression, body movement, eye contact. All those are essential if the contact were to be of any use. With solely verbal contact, misunderstandings could arise or difficulty in getting an idea or intention over correctly. I would certainly insist on video to ensure your ideas get over, and inversely of course," he paused for a moment, "I gather they have not yet tried to contact us?"

"Not to my knowledge, but that does not mean they haven't tried. There may be a technological gap between us. Petersen is attempting to contact them via the ISS right now. Very well, please contact General Carters here in the Whitehouse, inform him you are to oversee the First Contact protocol and when you have contact, inform me immediately."

"Eh Yessir, right away. I guess my fishing weekend is cancelled then?" he said with a weak smile.

"I think all our weekends are cancelled, M Cortez. Thank you."

Chapter 5

Taxies

"Fuck, what wrong with you Kowalski? You're sick," Chris said as he unmade his bed, strewn with ranking potatoes Kowalski had hidden under the sheets, a stench difficult to get rid of when it got into your nose. Everybody in the barracks was laughing as Chris backed away from his bed. Then suddenly a klaxon sounded off around the base and in their billings.

"What the fuck?" said Kowalski, covering his ears.

Then the loudspeakers came on. "Attention to all Space Guardians, we are now at DEFCON 2 and all Guardians are to meet in hall 21 for briefing by General Bastion immediately. Move!" said the sergeant over the speakers.

Everyone ran. Forty-five seconds later, the full contingent of Space Guardians were standing in line, at attention, questions written over their faces, electricity in the air.

A grim faced General Bastion came in and stood on the wooden podium, taped the microphone and said, "Ladies and Gentlemen. This is an emergency. This is not a drill. I repeat, not a drill. We have unidentified forces approaching earth on a thirty-degree angle north of the system's plane in the sector Ganymede minus 3.7. They will be here in three hours," he looked over the audience, "As we speak, three squadrons of F-15E Strike Eagles are landing here at Petersen. Each Guardian will take a seat in a fighter to Space Zero One, immediately. Take nothing with you. Your gear and suits are being prepared in Nevada, and the shuttles are undergoing take-off checklists at this very moment. One last word, those flyboys do not mess around with emergency take-offs. Do not let the Space Guardians down! Go! Go! Go!"

Everyone ran out the building toward the landing strip. "Fuck me," Kowalski shouted, running, as he saw a coordinated mess of F-15E's land and line up with their hatches opening one after the other. Ground teams were rushing toward them to open the ladders. "I'll take this one," Kowalski said to Chris, "Good luck mate and see you soon. Don't forget, no puking"

"I'll try but that spud stench is still following me around you shit," he smiled and waved, "Good luck."

Chris climbed the small ladder and, after several attempts, inserted himself into the rear seat of the jet. Once in, he buckled up, but the hood was coming down already and the plane was moving, motors roaring already as they fast taxied away from the other Jets. The pilot did not need a runway; fifty yards would do to get him up. Chris melded with his seat when the pilot put full throttle from a standstill. Immediately the Pilot operated the flaps and the F-15 made for a vertical take-off in anger. This was war, this was everything pushed to extreme limits. The nerve of the military, training clocking in, immediate and extreme action, no seconds lost, no chances taken. Chris looked out to shuddering skies. He'd put a bit of wood between his teeth and rode the rage, rode the wrath. Seconds later the plane levelled out but, just when he thought they were going into a cruise velocity, the pilot throttled forward with afterburner fury. Everything blurred, numbed, and became distant. The jet screamed through the air at Mach three. Four minutes later, the Pilot throttled off, the engine complaining at the aggression, spitting and blasting fire. Then he turned into a violent downward spiral to shake off velocity. The Jet sped downwards, excessively fast for Chris's liking. He was sure they were going to crash. This was it. A good life, short, but good. Thank you, God. He prayed as the ground sped up toward them in what he could only describe as a crash dive. Then at the last instant, the pilot levelled out, and before hitting the ground, hit full reverse thrust, producing a scream from Hell. Chris thought the Jet would explode into a fiery ball of atomised matter. The plane thudded hard onto the tarmac but remained down. The jet broke hard, smoke and fire bellowing from the wheels, and even a higher pitch scream came from the engines. Still moving fast, the jet veered off toward a designated area amongst other fighters who had just landed and spilled their sole occupants, dizzy, wavering and teetering as each of his companions left their jets. Relieved he was not the only one on the edge of sanity. He gingerly climbed down the ladder, took five steps away, turned to face the pilot, stood erect and gave a salute. The pilot, anonymous behind his visor, coolly turned his head, nodded and saluted in blood brother fashion. It fused them for life, Pilot and Space Guardian. Chris noted the name painted onto the fuselage, "Heaven's Hell" it read. They are gods, he thought. He turned and ran toward the building a hundred metres away.

Chris entered a small hanger he knew was the prep station. He would gear up and prepare for space flight with a specially designed suit and helmet for Space combat. Emphasis was on manoeuvrability and protection. The suits, pressurised with a web of flexible rubber tendons throughout with Kevlar titanium scales, glowing a golden grey as they glistened in the harsh lighting of the hanger. The suits were stealth, the scales would intermittently reflect signals in small haphazard flashes and would give few signs to any detection device. "I feel like a fish," Chris said, turning to Kowalski, who had just donned his suit.

"Yeah, I guess we'll be swimmin' soon. Batfish in the black!"

"Batfish in the black. That was quite good for you."

"Shut it and check my oxygen feeds," he grinned.

"They said around three hundred ships coming in, unbelievable. Can't see what we can do against that," said Chris.

Two techs came up to do a last check on the suits and help them load the straddles of explosives and ammunition that wore like a coat weighing them down. They also verified the thrust outlets for direction.

"Great, now I feel like a bear," Kowalski said, waddling towards the exit.

"We'll be alright once were up-"

The Sergeant interrupted him, crying out to everyone to hasten and move toward the open buses to take them to the two silos for launch.

The Shuttles, including the rockets and launchers, were imbedded in two separate silos one mile apart. A throwback to the shuttle space programme, appropriated and completely refurbished and updated. They had been on permanent readiness for several months now, and this was to be their maiden launch. Nasa oversaw the operations, and an army of techs ensured their viability for the declared parameters of their new job. Each shuttle held a squadron of twenty space Guardians in full combat gear. The cargo hold, modified to accommodate communication and armoury, was tight.

Their buses made the brief trip to the two silos, then the Guardians piled out and made their way to their designated shuttle. It was like walking onto a civil flight plane, but the doors and spaces between the seats were larger and no frills. Get in, strap up and pray. That was the mantra. The Guardians had ample training in space but used the one shot carrier rockets to get up and the ISS for a base until they descended in purpose-built capsules. It was all a bit Heath Robinson, but it worked and the Guardians had high expertise in space, albeit zero experience in fighting in such a strange environment. It will have to do.

"Here we go again," said Kowalski, who sat next to Chris.

"Yeah, those fighter pilots are the job, eh? Now the real deal. What was it? Mach Seven?"

"Yep, all the way up, into oblivion!"

"Nah, not oblivion, eternity!"

Warning came when the countdown begun. Everyone tensed, adrenaline swam through their bodies, the shuttle's commander threw a switch and all hell broke loose. First a deep roar which ran through their bones, then the shuddering, then the push, slight at first, amusing even, then it got serious, Mach one, Mach two, Mach three... a blur in front of

Chris's eyes, the seat in front of him wobbled, his hands clenched like vices to the armrests as the Rockets and booster shot the shuttle through the atmosphere like a bullet. Mach four, Mach five, Mach six, then the ride got smoother as it sped up to Mach seven, escape velocity. They heard and felt huge clashes and bumps as the rockets and boosters separated from the shuttle and the roar of its engines taking the load into space. Immediately, silence, calm and serenity took over the hold, a stark contrast to the din before. They were ghosts in the ether, spirits of death poised in cold space. Weightlessness took over like downing a cold beer on a hot day. Relief, appeasement and wakening. The Guardians' senses slowly coming back online. Functioning.

"Ok men," said the sergeant as he floated into the central area of the hold, "Stay put and buckled. According to intel, we have forty minutes before they arrive in orbit. I will go forward to our comms unit and determine out best approach vector. When the lights come on, helmet up, hook up your oxygen and gear up. Your rifles are loaded with the new zero recoil ammo. You will find them in front of you, if you hadn't noticed already. I will return with mission orders," he finished and floated off toward the front and entered the control cabin.

"I always like this, feeling light and airy. Space fairies!"

"Fairy my ass," said Kowalski, "What did he say, three hundred ships?"

"Yep, gonna be showdown if they want after us."

They waited in expectant silence for the sergeant to come back with orders. Hearts were throbbing within the hold, terror begat anger, begat determination, begat valour… the Space Guardians, primed and set, raged resolution to wreak havoc…

Chapter 6

First Contact

"Approaching earth orbit in twenty minutes, Sir," the navigation officer called out to Captain Ha'dok who was standing stoically on the bridge.

"Good. What do we have? Any defences or other vessels?"

"Apart from their Space Station, I detect only one vessel in proximity to the station and holding orbit in synch with it."

"Eh Sir," called out the comms officer, "We are being hailed by the station Sir," he turned and looked at the Captain expectantly.

"What are they saying?"

"They wish to communicate. They have detected us and are requesting a video feed."

"Video feed, hm, interesting. Very well. Don't answer for now. I will inform the Admiral. Navigation, hold the fleet's position. I will inform the Admiral personally," he said as he walked off the Bridge turning back to say, "M Zu'lu, you have the bridge."

Admiral Am'trach was savouring a Gratch, a refined alcohol, known for its calming qualities, when a knock came at his door. "Enter."

"Sir," the Captain said, "We are being hailed and they are requesting a video feed."

"Interesting, don't reply. I will come to the bridge."

A few minutes later, the Admiral came onto the Bridge and took his usual position set back from the Captain's post. "Very well, reply and say we agree to communication. Identify us."

"Very well Sir," said the comms officer, "This is the flagship Nau'tilous of the Cerulean fleet. Our Admiral will take your video feed in thirty seconds."

"This is the ISS, International Space Station. Thank you, we will put you through to the President of the United States of America. Please hold."

It took several minutes for the liaison to be made, then suddenly an elderly, yet smart man, sitting at a desk, came onto the screen. "Hello, my name is Peter Walters, I am the President of the United States of America. My people have invested me to liaise with you," Walters said, not with a little apprehension as he saw the image of the Admiral standing in his smart Green and blue uniform. Humanoid, yet different. Certainly not a hideous insect creature the President was dreading.

"Good day to you, Sir," said Am'trach, "My name is Admiral Am'trach. As you can see, we have arrived with a large fleet of our navy. We are a small part of the Cerulean

Navy which deals with new and wayward civilisations. Our role is to detect and evaluate the viability of any newly discovered civilisation for adhesion to the Cerulean directorate and eventually to the Consortium."

"Pleased to meet you, Admiral. Frankly, we were not aware of your existence. This is big news to us. What are you intentions?" the President asked.

"We have had time to evaluate your society and civilisation. It's values, how you treat each other and your motives of existence."

"Motives of existence?"

"Indeed, I am sure you have asked, what is the purpose of life? From what we can see from your history and present ideology, you are a race who seek to dominate your fellowman, destroy him if needs be, and manipulate others to obedience in favour of your Elites; governments and corporations. It would appear that your ruling class has surpassed its scope of action to ensure conformity from your populations. We have seen this in many countries on your planet. Governments, primarily, should exist to administer the population, to serve it. It would appear that you have inverted the roles and now the people are serving the government. Catering to your agendas and no longer for the betterment of the people. We deem this to be a product of both hubris and wickedness."

"I can assure you, Sir, that our Governments strive to ensure the safekeeping and well-being of their populations."

"Stop, we have seen your actions and the society you have set up, which are detrimental to the individual. Its enslavement, any sort of self-determination, long lost. Governments have taken the pedestal and have abused their position. We cannot let that happen. As is, your society is unfit for the Galaxy. There are principles you will need not only to understand but to adhere to, to be allowed to venture into our Spiral."

"You cannot let that happen? What do you mean? Who are you to think you can come here and dictate to us how to live our lives? I believe you have grossly misunderstood our society and how it works. It is imperfect, granted, but it's what we do, it's our home. We do not claim to be perfect, unlike your supposed Spiral dogma, nor do we take lightly to being bullied into submission. If fact, we do not do submission, Sir. As a civilisation, we will determine our own future and who we interact with."

"Our superiors have given us the authority and the power to stop any civilisation that we deem dangerous for our system."

"Who invested you?" interrupted the President.

"This Spiral arm's consortium of planetary governments. There is no higher authority."

"Well, Admiral, hear this, we do not recognise the legitimacy of your authority. We are independent and shall remain so. It's a shame our first meeting should be under such circumstances, but we shall not let you interfere with our planet. Is that understood?" Walters glared into the camera lens.

"As you wish Sir, we shall, nevertheless, cull your society so you don't represent a threat to the Spiral."

"What does that mean?"

"It means our fleet will do what it was designed to do. Farewell M President," he signed off with a smirk.

Chapter 7

Back at the office

"Well, that went well," Walters said to the many advisors, military and scientific staff clustered in his office. "They even spoke passable English."

M Cortez shuffled forward, "I would imagine that the officers of that fleet were all instructed to learn our language as part of their mission."

"Maybe so M Cortez, thank you," said the President.

"Fucking aliens," said General Carter. "Well done Sir, you showed them we are not a rollover." He glanced around the room, "Permission to go to DEFCON 1 Sir?"

He hesitated a millisecond, "Permission granted General. Enable." He said tiredly but determined. "Joanne, eh, Mrs Blaze, what's the situation with China and Russia?"

"They were listening in on your communication. I have confirmation that they will stand next to you in this conflict. They too have moved their systems up to full war alert."

"And our Space Guardians?" he looked at the General again, who was giving orders to up the DEFCON rating to its maximum level.

"In sit and ready," he said curtly.

"Ready? General, I don't think you understand. We are being threatened on our doorstep, the spectre of death and annihilation plane over our houses, our families, our children, who are defenceless. Our duty is to protect them by any means necessary. We are at war, General. I am chief of the Armed forces. I give you permission to shoot first, no quarter. Show them what we are made of."

"Yessir," gleamed the General, giving a salute and walking out of the office.

Chapter 8

Second contact (explosive)

Admiral Am'trach wiped his brow with his sleeve, "Strange people. They are wild and uncontrolled. We will never let them get into space," he said to Captain Ha'dok standing at his post, "Captain Ha'dok, please set the fleet in invasion formation. I want to see what these stupid beings do. It won't help them though," he said.

"Yessir, I will give orders immediately," the Captain moved over to the comms desk and conversed with the officer there.

The sensor operator suddenly jerked around on his swivel chair, "Sir, their vessel is moving toward us on our left flank. It's slow but gaining speed."

"Very well thank you," said the Captain, giving orders to create a group to detach from the fleet to meet them.

Both the Admiral and the Captain monitored the group's progress on the primary screen. When they were near the shuttle and had slowed down to a near stop, they exploded, one after the other. Within minutes, the group was decimated, flotsam upon the black of eternity.

"What happened?" the Admiral said, turning to the Captain.

"I don't know Sir, no shots were fired from their vessel," he turned toward the sensor operator, "Did you get any readings coming from their vessel, anything?"

"No Sir, no radio or weapons." He said thankfully, turning to his consol.

"We had a dreadnaught in that group, didn't we?" the Admiral asked.

"Indeed, we did-"

"Sir," interrupted the sensor operator, "We have a second vessel coming from our right flank, coming in fast."

Captain Ha'dok felt his hair raise upon his neck and a cold sweat creep through his body, "That was a decoy while the other ship came up to us. Comms, give orders to all ships to fire at will." It was too late.

The shuttle was hurtling into the right flank of the swarm and soon was amidst the floundering alien vessels. The seconds it took for them to receive orders to fire, the shuttle exploded into a ball of bright nuclear fire engulfing the whole of the hundred and twenty ships on that side of the fleet.

Admiral Am'trach was aghast, "What's happening Captain?"

"They blew up their own ship to destroy us!" he replied with wide unbelieving eyes locked onto the Admiral.

"Impossible, no one fights like that!"

Chapter 9

Semper Supra

Chris and Kowalski, who had made a two-man team like their teammates, thrust away from their target ship, leaving behind them two explosives stuck to the hull. One just behind what they deemed was the bridge and the second on the engine casing. They were set to explode simultaneously. They both flew to the next vessel and when out of range, Kowalski detonated the explosives, splitting the ship in two, evacuating the air and creating a miasma of fire and destruction. The fires didn't last long, just enough to burn up the oxygen in the vessel, but the blast ripped the ships apart. Chris saw other ships explode similarly within the fleet.

"Wow, now that was sweet," gloated Kowalski.

"I'm surprised we can sneak up to them like this, but we must be hard to detect. Ok, here's our next target. I'll go forward, you the engines," said Chris.

Forty Space Guardians had left both shuttles earlier and headed toward the swarm. The command team of one shuttle came over to the other and the pilot flew the empty shuttle, by remote, around orbit to come up on the other side of the fleet gaining tremendous speed as it flung itself off Earth's gravity well, in exponential acceleration. The fifty megaton nuclear bomb on-board was primed. When it flew into the midst of the right flank of the fleet, a weapons operator on the manned shuttle flicked a switch, detonating a nuclear blast which was seen from Earth. The damage was extensive.

The Guardians had made teams of two and flew via their inertia thrusts between the enemy vessels. Each time laying down explosives. The fleet was diminishing by the second, unable to detect the flitting Guardians in their stealth suites.

"Jones, Kowalski," a voice came over their comms breaking radio silence, "You are to meet up with Banks and Kruger. That Frigate your coming up on. We want it intact. That means boarding it. I am sending another six Guardians to assist you. Please proceed with haste before they hightail it out of here."

They both acknowledged and flew toward the vessel undetected. Banks and Kruger came up on their left flank, keeping their distance so as not to trigger the ship's sensors. Chris took command. "From what I can see, this vessel has two main entrances, one on each side. The bay's doors we can forget for the time being. I want those entrances blasted open. I'll go with Banks to the port-side, Kowalski and Kruger on the starboard, radio me when you are ready for detonation." Several minutes later, they all met over the top of the vessel, then Chris triggered the small explosives designed to rupture the hull plating around the doors. There was no noise, but the ship shuddered visibly as the weakened doors gave way to the pressure inside popping them like champagne bottles.

"Spectacular!" said Banks as he immediately made his way down the port-side again with Chris.

"This is it. No quarter, we take this ship," said Chris as they entered the hull through mangled plating and struts. Bodies were floating everywhere, ballooning without pressure. It was messy. "Right, toward the bridge," Chris said, gesturing to Banks. "Kowalski, make you way to the bridge as well. We take the bridge, we take the ship."

"Righto boss," said Kowalski as he positioned his rifle. Both teams had to make their way through tight, airless corridors open to space. Bodies floated eerily and silently. "This is too easy. I bet they weren't expecting that!"

"No, but be careful, were approaching the bulkhead doors leading to the bridge. It's locked," said Chris.

"Ours as well. They must have two entrances to their bridge on either side of the ship. Ok, Kruger, place those explosives and let's retreat."

The bridge doors disintegrated in unison as Chris triggered both sets of explosives. They had all retreated way back into the ship. The four Guardians floated toward the bridge, expecting resistance.

As they approached, gunfire rattled out from within. Chris, hiding around a large piece of plating which used to be a side panel for the Bridge, drew out his rifle and sprayed blindly into the area. He was thankful for the zero recoil ammunition designed specifically for weightless combat. Cries came from within as Kowalski and Kruger, on the other side, sprayed another shower of bullets, shattering monitors and equipment alike.

"Stop firing," cried Chris to the others. He then leaned in closer to the Bridge door, "Drop you weapons now!" he shouted. They couldn't hear the clatter of the guns dropping, but saw the alien's weapons float out of the wrangled doorway. Chris risked a look. Two survivors remained standing, not moving an inch. The other occupants of the bridge, strewn around the room in several splintered pieces with red blood flowing out of their bloated bodies. The two survivors had breathing apparatuses and suits. It was over. They had their first ship. A prize beyond value. Reinforcements came in through the wrecked hull and scoured the ship. No survivors.

A pilot came over from the nearby shuttle and, after some deliberation, started the engines and drew away from the main body of the fleet. He knew a storm was coming… Chris withdrew from the ship to make his solitary way toward the ISS. He wanted to be alone for a while. It never came easy to kill someone, even though he had the moral high ground. But he was part of a new force to defend Earth. Not as primarily thought, against other nations, but against foes from outer space. The attack gave him resolve. He would let nothing hurt Earth.

Chapter 10

The Mor'Dak rises

"Sir, they are boarding one of our vessels," said the captain.

"I can see that, Captain. Can we not blast that ship out of space? We can't let them capture one of our vessels. Think of the technology they'll get," said the Admiral.

"Unfortunately, our ships are too far away now, those that are still able. The others have been destroyed. I no longer see any explosions. Let's hope they have let off attacking us. This is horrendous. We don't even know how they are doing it."

"Stealth, Captain, Stealth. They came up to us with bodies, not vessels. Our sensors cannot detect them, more so if their suits reflect our probes. Also, ruse, remember that shuttle coming up over the horizon, sneaky but effective. What a mess. Captain, gather the fleet and retreat. I'm afraid we aroused the Mor'Dak from his pit this time."

"Yessir," the Captain turned to give withdrawal orders over the comms to the remainder of the fleet.

"How many did we lose Captain?"

"Out of the two hundred and ninety-eight vessels we started with, only seventy-one remain intact."

"Sir," the sensor operator spoke up nervously.

"What is it M Zak'ary?" shouted the Captain, a little too harshly.

"I am getting a reading of something coming our way from planet side. In fact, I am getting several. Velocities are Mach twelve and increasing," he turned to the Captain and the Admiral, both standing stock-still, "Missiles Sir, they're huge, almost the size of one of our Frigates!"

The Admiral shared a look with the Captain. Both knew.

Twenty-three Space proofed Ballistic Missiles, each armed with a fifty megaton warhead, bore toward the remains of the fleet at speeds beyond what the eye can follow. It was a coordinated hit by the USA, Russia and China. The scintillating maelstrom of nuclear fission lit up the solar system, competing with the sun for several instants. It left behind it a radioactive cloud of fused atoms; what remained of the Cerulean Fleet.

Half a hemisphere away, floating in space, Chris witnessed the nuclear destruction inflicted upon the unwary Aliens. He pondered the future for mankind in a Galaxy of fools. We will need courage and insight. His regard turned downwards. He smiled at the serenity he found. He would gladly give his life to safeguard his home, proud to be part of the Space Force, a Guardian of Earth.

Their motto? **"SEMPER SUPRA"**